I0640529

J.J. LORE

Evernight Publishing

www.evernightpublishing.com

Copyright© 2016

J.J. Lore

Editor: Karyn White

Cover Artist: Jay Aheer

ISBN: 978-1-77233-849-2

J.J. LORE

DEDICATION

This book is dedicated to the small town librarians who gave me the world when I was a child. They handed me books and I was able to travel to distant lands, ocean depths, and galaxies of the imagination. Thank you.

J.J. LORE

BEYOND LOVE

J.J. Lore

Copyright © 2016

Chapter One

Even though they were encased in wet slickers from neck to ankle, Teah Riuda knew they were Eleoni. There was something in the set of their shoulders, the confident swagger of their stride that was unmistakable and proclaimed they were the new law of the planet. She slowed her cart, the compulsion to get all the packages in her care back to the office tempered by the impulse to offer the new arrivals a ride into the settlement. It was raining terribly, as per usual on Rusk, so common courtesy inclined her to offer assistance since the path from the landing deck was long and treacherous in a downpour.

She coasted her hauler to a halt just beyond the two and turned in her seat to catch their attention. They stopped abruptly, the long, waterproof fabric of their coats swinging. Everything else was already soaking wet, courtesy of this planet's near incessant precipitation. The Eleoni were carrying long, hard-sided cases and had large duffels slung over their shoulders. One was a striking woman with high cheekbones and dark hair slicked back in a tight tail while the man beside her possessed a short beard and coils of long hair circling his head. Both had light eyes paired with caramel skin, and shared similar facial features.

Teah couldn't restrain her smile of welcome. She was glad to see them, whoever they were, because their arrival signaled the start of the formal annexation of Rusk. All the unruly inhabitants had grown even more rowdy since the death of the district circuit marshal a month before. She was looking forward to calm and order. It would make delivering mail so much easier.

"Hello. Could I offer you a ride into town?"

The woman smiled at her offer, but the bearded man stepped forward with a slight scowl. "Are you the postal officer?"

She nodded, a bit taken aback by his apparent displeasure.

"Then you should be well aware it is against regulations for you to transport passengers while you are conveying unsecured material." His violet eyes flashed hot, and she started with the rebuke.

"I know. I just…" She stammered to a halt, simultaneously embarrassed at her careless disregard for her duties and offended that her attempt to be welcoming was rebuffed. Many of her fellow humans held the opinion that Eleoni were arrogant and controlling, illustrated by how quickly they'd taken possession of this planet after a protracted legal dispute between them and the Kotze, the other race settling here. Judging by how instinctively this one had put her in her place, there might be some truth to it.

"Why do you chastise her, Eidan? Would you arrest her for being polite?" The woman stepped forward with a sizeable grin. "I'm Brida Cozad, deputy sheriff, and I'm happy for the accommodation. I've never been one to allow a line in the code keep me from comfort. Thank you."

She dropped her duffel in the bed of the cart and then carefully wedged the rectangular case alongside. With a grunt, she hoisted herself up to the seat next to Teah, careful not to brush her with her wet overcoat.

"Will you join us, Sheriff?" Brida's voice was filled with what, in a human Teah would call amusement, but since her sole face-to-face experience with Eleoni had been a job interview with one bored woman, she couldn't be sure.

As Teah waited, she inspected the new territorial sheriff, starting with his heavy leather boots sunk in the muck of the path. The footgear was expensive-looking and highly polished, but already mud encrusted from the short walk he'd taken from the port landing deck. The boots remained still. What sort of man would walk a kilometer in a downpour rather than accept a simple ride? She and these two law enforcement officers were on the same side, both in the service of the new allied government now controlling this world. A sudden jolt of outrage filled her, and she looked up to find him frowning even as droplets of rain rolled down his cheeks.

Without really thinking about the consequences, she activated the forward momentum of the vehicle and rolled it away from him. Just before directing her attention to the trail ahead, she saw Eidan's eyes widen and his mouth open as if to speak. Too late, they were already sliding away. Brida chuckled next to her and grabbed hold of the roll bar overhead.

"What's your name, brave human?"

Awareness of how stupid she'd just been chilled her blood more than the damp air she was breathing in ever had. "Teah Riuda, lead postal officer. Why do you call me brave?"

"My brother Eidan, you'll come to learn, is quite sure he always knows best. It's one of the reasons he's so suited to law enforcement. He's not used to anyone, how shall I put it, thwarting him."

The deputy's raised eyebrows would have been comical in another circumstance, but Teah know she was in trouble. She wracked her brain for the specifications of the regulations she'd just violated. "Will he really arrest me?"

"Since we haven't even located our jail yet, he doesn't exactly have a place to put you, does he?"

Brida was funny. Too bad her brother was a humorless stick. "So I'm safe for the moment. It would probably be foolish of me to drop you off there when we get into town, wouldn't it?"

"I have no intention of locking you up, at least not for such a minor lapse. Then again, Eidan might decide to arrest me for dereliction of duty. We could be cellmates!" Brida leaned back in her seat and propped her muddy boots against the side of the cart. They were on a steeper slope now, and Teah had to guide the vehicle more carefully through some minor slips and slides. "It's my understanding Rusk harbors criminals of much more serious intent. I'll save my energy for more challenging situations."

"It's a little rough around the edges." That was as far as she was prepared to describe at this point. Humans were the interlopers on this planet, possessing none of the rights of the two alien species who had sovereignty to co-govern Rusk. The Kotze concentrated on their mining efforts and seemed happy to leave all other aspects of creating civilization to their 'til now absent Eleoni partners. This left humans to wander in and take up the slack of providing various services, all of which had been unrestrained until a few weeks prior, after the annexation. Many folk were criminals now, between the unregulated distilleries, gambling rings, and psychotropic substances.

People had been grudgingly accepting of her presence as well as the official medical team when they'd arrived a few months before. Most appreciated the idea of getting their shipments in a reliable way and having someone around who could set a broken bone or provide some relief from foot rot. Alien police intent on enforcing taxation and putting the kibosh on a lot of questionable revenue streams, on the other hand, weren't going to be welcomed with open arms.

"Eidan will grind them down, with my able assistance, of course."

Her easy, almost smug, confidence reminded Teah of the fact she'd managed to ignore for a few seconds. She'd engaged in a slight impropriety with the new sheriff and then driven off with his deputy. There would likely be repercussions. The palms of her hands prickled as she considered this, so she tightened her grip on the steering rod, sure she didn't want to drive off the side of the trail.

Teah glanced at the Eleoni woman and found she was studying the road ahead, looking for all the galaxy as if she was on a pleasure ride rather than descending into a roiling pit of immorality.

****

Nothing was as it should be. Eidan Cozad knew he needed to calm down and approach the situation with some dispassion, but it seemed as soon as he'd arrived in Rusk every subsequent event conspired to emphasize how far he'd fallen, how difficult it was going to be to crawl back up. The security facility was shabby and slack, the unrelenting precipitation was already depressing him, Brida was smirking far too much, and then there was the human element. The Kotze didn't concern him at all for he had much experience with their ways, but exiled Earthers were a new experience.

He'd sensed the hostility from the human deputies lounging around the station, and there had been that shocking breach of protocol with the postal officer. Eidan's shoulders tensed when he thought about her, thought about how he'd behaved. No, thought about how *she'd* behaved. She'd made an offer he was duty-bound to refuse, then had flinched and blinked her eyes like he'd been in the wrong for pointing it out. Just as he'd reconsidered the issue, she'd boldly driven off with his sister, leaving him to trudge through mud for a kilometer while lugging twenty kilos of vital gear. He'd already reprimanded his sister for leaving his side. She was assigned to be his bodyguard after all. She'd been unrepentant and snappish, still smarting from her recent loss of meld with a high status Eleoni marine. He was sympathetic to her plight, since being separated from the person you'd bonded with was a torment, both emotionally and physically. But she'd made that sacrifice for him, which inclined him to be very tolerant whenever she lost her temper.

He and Brida had put in a long day organizing supplies at the station, directing the human officers to clean it from top to bottom. Eidan had recalibrated the locking mechanisms and added his and his sister's tracking codes to the operating system, all while suffering through the intermittent interruptions of civilians stopping by to stare at their new overlords. The humans would mutter under their breath, and a few reluctantly returned his salutations with a sloppy rejoinder. Now it was time to retrieve some of their belongings they'd shipped ahead. This meant he and his sister were now walking along an uneven sidewalk toward the post office where he'd have to encounter the light-haired woman with the big brown eyes, again. The *postal officer*, rather.

Instead of dwelling on the awkwardness to come, he decided to survey his new posting. Rusk was not an impressive settlement. As an unregulated outpost, it stood to reason that it wouldn't be a well-planned and sanitary place, but the level of grime, disorder, and structural flaws surrounding them surprised him. Ramshackle modular units ranging from arctic survival tubes to inflatable escape pods had been thrown up and tied down next to generic modular units intended for refugee resettlements, along with buildings cobbled together from castoff ship parts and discarded packing materials. He wouldn't hazard a guess as to what sorts of enterprises filled some of them, but the bars, mercantile establishments, and brothels were easy to pick out.

The haphazard variety of Rusk's limited architecture was matched by the town's denizens. Numerous Kotze clad in heavy jumpsuits lugged digging supplies, a few nervous-looking Ra'uf, and scores of chattering humans swarmed the filthy streets and alleys. All signs pointed to this being the back end of beyond, exactly where his superiors wanted him to be.

"So what do you think of all your beloved humans? They look much less impressive than I was expecting." Brida widened her eyes for effect.

"They aren't my *beloved*. They are much frailer than the pictures indicated. And more disorganized." He'd taken one human culture class while at university, but hadn't anticipated ever encountering them in any numbers until his superiors decided his zeal for investigation hit a bit too close to home at headquarters. He'd put together a comprehensive report on which of his fellow officers were stealing luxury goods out of evidence, and that signaled the end of his tenure in Eleoni special services. Within a month he was conveniently transferred to a faraway planet where his curiosity and willingness to question the status quo wouldn't put his superiors in an awkward position.

Brida nodded greetings to all who met their gazes, and Eidan was grateful his sister had assumed the more sociable role. It gave him time to strategize. She halted abruptly and Eidan wondered for a moment if she'd stumbled on a tilted plank, but when he followed her line of sight, he understood.

Across the puddle-filled street stood a small, bright yellow building. Wide windows graced the façade and framed a bold blue door. The color scheme was a dead giveaway. This was the official Collective postal office. Its appearance was like a tiny sliver of home wedged in the middle of chaos. Eidan knew it was a new structure since mail service had only begun on Rusk five months before, but he was still impressed by how clean it was. Someone must spend at least an hour a day clearing away mud spatters and buffing out gouges made by careless passers-by hauling mining equipment.

A tickle of unease wandered around in his gut. He was only moments away from encountering the human woman, Teah Riuda, as Brida had informed him, and he wondered how this interaction might proceed. His sister didn't even pause before plunging into the street, dashing between two heavy-duty carts heading in opposite directions, a fine spray of mud filling the damp air as they accelerated. He followed more cautiously. It wouldn't do for the sheriff to incite a vehicular collision within hours of arriving on planet.

His sister had already disappeared inside by the time he reached the door and as he entered, a gentle chime sounded. Walking in the post office was like coming home. All the standard features—green tiled walls, black resin counter, tiny silver doors securing personal boxes arranged in neat rows—everything resembled the post office he'd gone to as a child, all the ones he'd encountered all over Eleon, and those located on more far-flung worlds.

Brida leaned on the counter talking with the woman in question. The postal officer was younger than she'd appeared that morning while swathed in waterproof fabric, at least as far as he was able to evaluate human physiology. An amused grin curled her lips as she listened to Brida spin a charming tale, but as soon as she spotted him approaching, she straightened her posture and smoothed the front of her tunic. The gesture brought his gaze to her torso, and he nearly stumbled as he noticed her breasts. Of course, he'd known she would possess those secondary sex characteristics, but the concealing raingear she'd worn earlier had lulled him into forgetting about them. He should ignore them; staring was rude. Why had the postal service issued a uniform top that so blatantly emphasized such beautifully-shaped features?

Embarrassment made him clear his throat as he stopped at Brida's side. Perhaps his sister had already made the arrangements for delivery of their goods, and he could simply stand quietly and not make it too obvious he wasn't looking at the human woman. Teah narrowed her eyes and inclined her head to look *him* up and down, finally bringing her gaze to lock with his. Her eyes were a rich coppery brown and as deep as a quiet forest pool. His muscles twitched, and he fought his sudden inclination to turn on his heel and exit the place.

She sighed deeply, and the sound buzzed in his ears longer than it should have. A sharp prod from Brida brought him out of his daze, and he turned on his sister with a frown.

"You're making a muck of it."

Eidan didn't understand how Brida could have picked up on his worry about dealing with this woman again. He'd made a great effort not to refer to her, or his stiff behavior, for the entire day.

"The floor, you're making a mess," his sister continued, and with a start, Eidan looked down to see he'd tracked slimy mud all over the clean green tile floor. A glance back at the door revealed his dirty path, as well as Brida's discarded footwear stationed on a shallow tray obviously intended for that purpose.

The apology he should have said stuck in this throat like an amphibious tick, so instead of croaking and hacking, he shut his mouth and walked back to the door where he tottered foolishly as he pulled off his tall boots. Avoiding the smears of mud, he returned to the counter only to find Teah retreating out of sight behind a wall of shelves stuffed with battered shipping cases and sealed packages. The postal uniform, unfortunately, was also quite flattering to her round buttocks. *Don't look.*

Brida quirked an eyebrow at him and stroked one finger along her chin. "She doesn't seem to like you much."

"Why does that matter? It's a simple transaction. We're only here to retrieve our property, and she's required by law to hand it over." As he said the words, the young woman emerged from a smallish door and bustled out with a mop and bottle. She must have heard his statement because she sniffed and ostentatiously began to spray cleanser over the mess on her floor, the foaming liquid coming perilously close to his sock-covered feet. As she began to scrub the tiles with her mop, she spoke up, her voice strained, perhaps by the effort she was putting into cleaning.

"I assure you, Sheriff Cozad, I don't wish to retain your shipments any longer than necessary. If only you had thought to bring a cart along, I'd be able," she paused for breath, the wet strands of the mop almost curling around his feet, "to get my back room cleared of thirty percent of its backlog."

She brought her mop around to parade rest position and issued a credible glare at him. Eidan repressed his urge to step back, away from the menace of the muddy mop and the challenge in her stare. He was the sheriff of an entire planet, and one postal officer with a hygiene mania wasn't going to be even a footnote in his day. Brida broke the tension when she laughed, and both he and Teah Riuda whipped their heads around to level stares at his sister. She held up her hands and shuffled on stocking feet to the door.

"I'm off to commandeer a vehicle, Sheriff." With that, Brida scooped up her muddy boots and made her escape outside, leaving Eidan alone with Teah. With another sniff, the postal officer marched back to the entrance to the counter and snapped it closed behind her. The click of a locking mechanism was loud in the quiet of the now-deserted post office. Just as he was contemplating donning his own boots and taking a stroll around the rest of Rusk to orient himself, she popped up behind the counter, a slight flush of pink on her cheeks.

"I'd offer to take you to the storage room to start going over your shipments, but regulations state only bonded Collective employees are allowed in the secured area." She arched her slender eyebrows at him. So she was trying to one-up him with her security clearance?

Without a word, he reached into his jacket pocket and pulled out his PD. She blinked once and then retrieved a glove scanner from under the counter, collecting his personal data with a quick wave of her fingertips and flash of light. She squinted at the reader on the wrist and nodded her head once as his details apparently checked out. She again disappeared behind the wall, and he heard the door click open. He stepped over to it, mindful not to slip on the wet floor.

The storage space was as tidy as the public area. Shelves ran from floor to ceiling and were filled with all manner of oddly shaped packages in a variety of sizes. He didn't spot her in the vicinity so continued on toward the back of the building, passing through another open doorway into a much larger space. Here were the big shipments, sturdy resin crates the size of large pieces of furniture, huge cylinders containing who knew what sort of object. The air smelled slightly of machine lubricant and damp paper. As he walked further in, he spotted Teah studying a readout on a monitor located next to a small heater. Parked on either side of the unit were two soft chairs. A small box containing wads of thick thread and some lethal-looking sticks sat between them. Her head was bent down as she concentrated on her task and he couldn't help but notice how she had her light brown hair pulled up, exposing her slender neck. A little warning pinged deep in his brain.

"My last tally for you and your deputy was twenty-one individual shipments. Does that correlate with your records?" She was all business as she turned to face him, her glove scanner at the ready. He had no idea how many packages and bundles Brida had sent ahead. He'd merely piled up what he'd wanted in the middle of the floor and it disappeared every time she'd left his apartment on Eleon. He vaguely remembered agreeing to some furniture pictured on a shopping display, but beyond that, all those details were part of Brida's responsibility. She'd taken on the minutiae of their move in an effort to distract herself from the morass of fluctuating hormones her lost meld had left her. Eidan had handled all the bureaucratic necessities before their demotion, or "transfer to adventure" as his sister mocked it. As he admitted he didn't know how many packages awaited, the post officer exhaled through her nose and tilted her head.

"I thought you were—never mind." She closed her eyes for a pained second, then regarded him again.

"You thought I was what?"

Her lips tightened. "Brida indicated you were a very organized and efficient individual."

She *was* chastising him. How unique. "I am."

Again she quirked her eyebrow, clearly skeptical. "I suppose you'll have to trust me to account for these items correctly. I'd hate for you to think I lost something or misplaced it. Then you'd have to make a return visit. Inefficient use of your time and all that."

Eidan stared at her, hoping his features weren't betraying the mixture of irritation and amusement ricocheting inside him. This human woman was quite bold. "We can't have that. In the interest of speeding this process along and allowing me to leave you in peace, I shall call my deputy and ascertain how close she is to arriving."

Teah gave him a curt nod and indicated a wide door leading out of the building. It clanked open as she hit a button on the wall and he stepped out on a small loading dock sheltered by an overhang. He was facing a narrow alley strewn with all sorts of debris and smelling of burning fuel and something that had died a few days ago. It was still raining.

At his summons, Brida answered and declared she was close but currently hemmed in by two vehicles that had attempted to pass on the main thoroughfare and were now stuck in the mud. Eidan sighed and assured her he'd wait. It had been a long and tiring day, and the thought of finally making their way to their yet-unseen house filled him with longing, although the idea of unpacking was unappealing. Perhaps he could maneuver Brida into doing it. He wanted a shower, a meal, and a bed in that order.

Just as he realized his bed was currently compressed in a tube stashed in the storage space behind him, a battered cart rolled around the corner, Brida at the drive rod grinning like she'd won the Solar Flare Race. She pulled it to a halt at the loading ramp, waves of mud swelling around the vehicle's knobbed tires. His sister waved and swung out of the driver's side, neatly leaping to the dock and avoiding getting her boots dirty. Eidan stood by, hampered by his lack of footwear, as his sister and Teah efficiently loaded the cart's hauler bed with a plethora of goods. It seemed Brida had shipped enough material to furnish not only their new residence, but several others besides. The two chatted easily with each other, and Eidan struggled with a bit of envy. Brida was the charming one, able to negotiate with a panicked thief or talk down a tense situation while leaving Eidan to play the heavy. It was good camouflage for his sister since she was actually the more skilled and ruthless fighter.

Just as the two finished tying down the mound of boxes and crates with some heavy-duty elastic straps, a human appeared in the alley and approached with a purposeful stride. Eidan supposed it took a purposeful stride to make any headway in the muck. The stranger was wearing several layers of loose clothing, all of them wet and mud spattered. He had a greying grizzle on his uncovered head and sharp black eyes peering from his wizened face. With a cry and a wave of his arm he hailed Teah, and she greeted him with a brief word.

"The name's Bokum. Provisional mayor of Rusk," he announced with a genial tone, but Eidan wasn't swayed. He'd already read a preliminary report about the state of his new jurisdiction, necessarily brief due to the lack of official documents, but Bokum had managed a mention. The human now standing in front of him, grimacing out an insincere smile, ran one of the largest protection rackets on the planet. Provisional mayor was the self-appointed and polite title for the man who wielded a lot of sordid power in this small community.

Eidan accepted the human's handclasp because it was polite. Brida followed suit and drifted over to stand at Eidan's right shoulder in a basic protective posture. Teah stayed back within the frame of the open door, her dark eyes flickering between the mayor and him.

"Just wanted to introduce myself. In an informal way, you understand. Welcome you to our town." Bokum's clipped sentences matched the sharp curiosity gleaming in his eyes. Eidan thanked him and held his tongue, intrigued by what this obviously cunning man was actually aiming at.

Bokum planted his feet and wedged his hands on his hips as he threw out his chest. "Things work a little different here outside the bounds of the Collective. Lots of adjustments for everyone now, with the arrival of the good guys." He snickered.

Eidan nodded once. "I'm sure the population of Rusk is eagerly anticipating all the benefits that accrue to citizens of our government. For those that apply for the privilege."

Bokum tilted his head like he was considering this. Eidan had his doubts about the man's sincerity. "Benefits, sure. But also disadvantages that'll make plenty of good folks unhappy. I hate to see that."

The idea that order, civility, and reliable food inspectors would distress a law-abiding person was laughable. "Disadvantages?"

The smaller man wrinkled his face. "Change is hard for folks. Riles things up, and people get nervous. I imagine the same goes for your kind."

Eidan waited a beat for Bokum to actually explain what sort of down side there was to being a citizen of the Collective, but none was forthcoming. Brida discreetly flexed her arms and glanced around the alley almost as if she was expecting a surprise attack. Eidan figured it would take at least a few more days on planet before they provoked some sort of violent backlash. "Eleoni have varying opinions when it comes to progress."

Brida gave him a sidelong glance at this massive understatement. The more conservative factions on his planet would be entirely content to load the inhabitants of Rusk into a freight hauler and then incinerate the entire town to start it over in Eleon fashion. His own views were far more progressive.

Eidan noticed Teah shifting from foot to foot. She seemed tense from her tight shoulders down to her clasping hands. There was something amiss in this situation for her, but he couldn't hazard a guess.

"Not so familiar with your species. Only seen a few and they were pretty standoffish. I expect nothing less from the lawgivers. Probably going to be a lot more stringent than our late, lamented marshal." Bokum narrowed his eyes as he studied both him and Brida. "You're untouchable when you make all the rules."

Eidan knew his brow was creeping up with a blend of curiosity and skepticism as well as appreciation for the other man's acumen. He wondered if humans had an equivalent expression. "Rules?"

The provisional mayor blew a breath out between his pursed lips, almost whistling. "Sure. What's right, what's wrong, what's allowed as long as you keep it on the quiet. How you'll pay if you get caught. How to get off if bad luck befalls you. All those rules."

Eidan nodded. He suspected that Bokum wasn't merely having a philosophical discussion out here in the misty alley. "Lucky for all of us there's little ambiguity in the laws I'm here to see enforced."

Bokum regarded him steadily. "I see. Your certainty might be tested out here. Pretty isolated outpost, you know. But I should be welcoming you. Feel free to contact me if you need any sort of advice or service. I make it my business to be as helpful as possible."

Helpful at a steep price, Eidan was sure. Feeling like the provisional mayor's attempts to ascertain if he was bribable had taken up enough of his time, Eidan drew in a deep breath and again held out his hand. This was the way humans began and ended conversations, so he hoped the non-verbal communication was effective in this instance. Bokum opened his mouth as if to say more, then twisted it up into a scowl as he shook hands. The man made an insincere farewell, then stomped back down to the alley where his attempt to stride away was hampered by the sticky road surface.

"Sounds like we were issued a bit of a challenge," Brida said.

"And a bit of a warning." He didn't appreciate that reference to Marshal Phelen. The woman had been found dead in an alley and the rudimentary autopsy the clinic had performed hadn't detected signs of unnatural death, but he had his suspicions.

Eidan again found his gaze easing Teah's way. At some point she'd gone back into the interior of the post office and retrieved his boots. She held them extended from her side to prevent any chance of mud finding her well-tailored and clean uniform.

"Thought I'd save you a trip back inside," she said as she handed them over. Eidan suppressed the urge to ask her if she was trying to hurry him along out of her sight. He hadn't been that rude by Eleoni standards, but perhaps humans had lower thresholds. His professor hadn't delved deep enough, it seemed. He was going to get a crash course on the finer points cross-cultural relations in his time here.

****

Teah smiled and nodded at all the appropriate moments as she listened to her friend's long story about some tipsy Kotze in from the diggings to gamble at his table, but her mind could barely keep track between delivering packages, walking along the slippery walkway, and *not* thinking about Eleon men.

"So I'm keeping track of the speed roller as I do, and almost miss it when one of the Kotze pulls a blade and tries to stab his buddy. I yelled for help from Pico, but there was yellow blood everywhere by the time she got there to break it up. That hematoglobin stains." Dorian Larwood shook his head as he likely contemplated his upcoming laundry bill, his genetically modified eyes blinking rapidly.

"I'm surprised. I always thought Kotze got along with each other so well. All that consensus and shared property," Teah said as she dropped a flat package off in the Stardawn Lounge's mail slot. Most of the entertainment businesses weren't open when she did her morning run, so they'd cut holes in their walls to accommodate hand deliveries. Nothing too sophisticated, but so far, the method was working. She hoped to convince residents to install security panels, but those cost money most bartenders and brothel runners were unwilling to spend.

"They get along when they haven't been drinking and are worn out from mining." Dorian said with a grin. "Get 'em in town and liquored up and it's another story."

"Then I guess it's a good thing we're getting our new law enforcement set up. I heard another shipload of them is on its way." She searched her hand cart for the next delivery.

"Are you serious? The Collective and those Eleoni are the worst thing that's happened to Rusk since last year's parasitic syphilis outbreak." Dorian looked up and down the street, not spotting too many pedestrians since most residents were sleeping it off. He was still too energized from his late shift at the Take Your Chance Parlor to relax, which was why he liked to accompany her on her morning rounds.

Teah found the smallish box she was looking for and held it up for a scan to verify the address. Dorian, who was pacing a couple of meters away, nodded his head.

"You got it, some sort of medication for Lolly Moreo."

"Dorian! You're not supposed to read that. It's confidential." Teah was aghast at her mistake. She knew her friend's eyes had been enhanced through gene therapy so he could keep track of all the moving pieces in the games he ran, but he knew better than to be nosy about her deliveries. "You're so good at this, you ought to take the exam for Collective service."

Her friend cackled and held up his hands like she was going to take a swing at him. "There's no way I'd sign on to be some government hand. So many rules, so much pressure to behave, and having to bow down to those superior Eleoni on top of it? I mean, who burned in orbit and left them in charge of the galaxy? Besides, I make more money at the Last Chance than I can spend. What am I going to buy anyway? A new shovel or a big old coral ball?"

Teah laughed. It was true. Retail options were sparse in Rusk. That's why she'd recently placed an order for some new clothes from a merchant several solar systems away, and was expecting the delivery with the next incoming ship. Just thinking about how much of her newly-earned money she'd spent was enough to make her move quickly to her next stop and begin working again.

"Speaking of superior Eleoni, look who's up early and on the prowl," Dorian said under his breath as they resumed the route. Teah didn't have to look up. She'd been aware they were close to the security office and had been vigilant about *not* looking in that direction as they'd drawn closer. She didn't want another encounter with the sheriff so soon after yesterday's debacles. Her cheeks flushed hot as she remembered how many faux pas she'd committed. She risked a glance across the street and saw him leaning against a railing in front of his building. He was dressed in the full colonial law enforcement uniform, deep blue jacket and trousers, metallic red buttons and braid, and colorful insignia she couldn't interpret. His eyes were obscured by the peaked cap he wore, so she wasn't sure where he was looking. Not at her, she hoped.

"I know we're supposed to be open-minded and welcoming, but I think they're weird looking," Dorian said, as Teah slipped Lolly's delivery into the drop box bolted beside the older woman's front door. "Mostly it's the eyes. I mean the purple and yellow really throw me off. Not normal. And their skin. Have you heard they're striped?"

Teah scoffed, both because she didn't find the Eleoni's appearance off-putting, and at the absurd notion their fellow humanoids were so decorated under their clothes. Thinking about an Eleoni, like Eidan Cozad, for instance, without his clothes was unprofessional. But now that she'd considered it, she was finding it difficult to halt her speculation. He looked very solidly-built, and those lips framed by the beard seemed fuller and softer than they should. "What about spots? Maybe they have spots. Or scales?"

Dorian rolled his eyes as they continued down the walk. Should she wave at the sheriff? Acknowledge his presence in some way? Indecision made her hands clammy. She managed to look at him as they passed by, and he responded to her chin dip with one of his own. Sighing out a breath of relief, she was happy to listen to Dorian as he chattered about one his fellow dealers who'd had some sort of seizure the night before. Dorian suspected it was brought on by a new array of pulsing lights the owner of the Last Chance had just installed. Anyone with modified eyes was susceptible to such incidents, but it seemed as if Dorian's supervisor didn't much care. Her friend recounted the incident in a light tone, but worry underlay his words.

"How long do you think they'll last?"

"If it was up to me, I'd be cutting the power source immediately." Teah was worried for her friend's safety. Having some workplace safety laws applied in Rusk would be a wonderful thing, just so situations like this wouldn't exist.

"No, I mean the Eleoni." Dorian pursed his mouth and gave her an impatient glance.

Teah paused her little follow-me cart. It was nearly empty and had been bouncing on the uneven surface in an alarming way. "Why would they leave? They just got here."

Dorian shrugged his shoulders. "It's not too friendly of a place for them, is it? Rusk is nearly all Kotze and humans, so it's not like they've got a lot of allies here. We humans are the majority in town, and lots of us feel that law enforcement should have stayed in our hands with our late marshal. It's our people after all, and we understand each other better than an Eleoni ever would."

"Do you think there's going to be trouble?" Teah couldn't stop the question from bubbling out. The arrival of Eidan and Brida helped legitimize her position since all three of them were representatives of Collective civil service, her human status notwithstanding. She'd been nervous ever since the death of Phelen, and had been breathing easier since the sheriff and his deputy were planetside.

"Of course there is. This town is brimming with grievances and those two aliens haven't even started enforcing their new laws yet." Dorian paused for a moment, his mouth curled up in a cynical line. "Do you really think our illegitimate town fathers are going to simply bow out and conform to Eleoni dictates?"

A shiver of unease worked under her skin. She'd been on planet only a few months whereas Dorian had been here since the beginning. Her friend was also in the know regarding most of the now illegal activities of Rusk. If he thought there was danger, she believed him.

"Besides, they aren't going to want to stay when they find out the mounts at Gregor's Pleasure Spread are boycotting."

Teah stumbled to a halt, all thought of completing her route now completely absent from her shocked brain. A brain suddenly imagining the sheriff naked and rhythmically straining for an orgasm as sweat slicked his skin. "They aren't going to have sex with them?"

Dorian shook his head, his eyes wide. "I've heard from several there wasn't enough money in the galaxy. Gregor's not happy, but considering there are only a few even on the planet, it's not like he's losing out on a big income stream. Yet."

Teah pretended to search in her bag as she processed this. Gregor's staff were well-trained professionals. What would be holding them back? She'd never heard of the sex workers practicing their trade with the Kotze, but she'd assumed that was because the diggers were very unrestrained amongst themselves and didn't harbor any sort of pent-up energy in that area. What she'd seen of Eidan, and the few others of his race she'd encountered, conformed to human physiology very closely. "Eleoni and humans are nearly genetically identical."

"You wouldn't think that half a chromosome would matter so much, would you? But it does. I just can't imagine getting naked with an entirely different species." Her friend glanced back the way they'd come. "The sheriff's still out there."

Now she really didn't want to walk back to the post office. "He's vigilant. That's his job."

Chapter Two

Exhaustion crept into Eidan's muscles and bones like a sluggish malaise. He and Brida had been putting in eleven hour shifts, alternating with each other as they got to know the town and their fellow peace officers. So far, they'd received a chilly reception from nearly everyone, and he was coming to the conclusion at least half of the human staff would have to go. Poorly trained, unmotivated, uncooperative, and he had dire suspicions most were corrupt. The circuit marshal had obviously spent little time with her staff.

It was late evening, the perpetual rain was thundering on the roof of their new house, and he was desperate for some sleep before he had to get up and do it all over again. He looked around for anything that should be stowed before he stumbled to bed. Brida had done a good job setting up the place, even if it was under duress, lots of comfortable furniture, well-stocked kitchen, and a much appreciated sauna. Sharing a home with his sister had become comfortable almost immediately, and he was grateful she'd transferred with him, as was their family. It hardly seemed like an exile from all that was sophisticated and pleasant when he was in their home, but as soon as he stepped outside his fate was clear in every spatter of mud and unfriendly look flung his way.

A chime from the door alert sounded, and he strode to the closest security monitor. To his shock, Teah's face, framed by a dripping hood, gazed right at the lens he'd thought he'd concealed very well in the doorframe outside. A shiver of hot and cold cascaded along his nerves, and he wondered if it was dread or anticipation. In either case, he was still compelled to invite her in.

He opened the door, very aware she was the first visitor to step foot into his new home. She stood just inside the door as he closed out the rain and dark, her slicker dripping on the absorbent mat under her muddy boots. There were tiny droplets on her pinked cheeks. He tried to remember what humans traditionally did to welcome someone.

"Are you thirsty?" A stupid question, she was covered in water.

She shook her head and tightened her lips. "No one knows I'm here, but I couldn't stay away any longer. I've been thinking about this for days." The words tumbled out in a breathy rush.

Eidan wasn't sure what she meant by that. She licked her lips and stared at him like he was the most fascinating thing she'd ever seen. An enticing tickle of an idea entered his head. Was she offering some sort of clandestine sexual encounter? Human women were reportedly difficult to read when it came to sexual invitations or lack thereof. Eidan had never actually met anyone who'd managed coitus with a human, or at least no one had confessed to such.

"I'm in a tough position."

He was, too. Just the stray thought of sex with her evaporated all his fatigue in a warm rush of readiness. He'd heard humans were casual in their sexual pairings with no burden of a potential meld to restrain them, but hadn't anticipated a coupling would present itself so soon in his tenure. Not wanting to say anything that would betray his uncertainty, he stayed silent and watched her as she took in a shallow breath.

"Why am I doing this?" she whispered, then covered her face with her hands as she let out a little moan. Not an especially seductive move, but perhaps this was some variant he hadn't studied. First, he needed to get her out of that wet and concealing overcoat, and then they could discover how relations might progress.

"Allow me to hang up your outer garment."

With a huffed breath she pulled her hands away from her cheeks and fumbled with the catches of her coat. "I'm sorry. I'm dripping all over your carpet."

"That is the purpose of the mat."

Once they managed to rid her of the slicker, he hung it up on a hook by the door and turned back to find her standing stock still on the rug, her arms stiff at her sides and her eyes wide as she took in the room around her. She was wearing a casual version of her uniform. It fit as close as the other and now that they were in more private surroundings he felt more comfortable assessing her full breasts and curving hips. Yes, if he cared to undertake coitus with a human, Teah would make a good partner.

"Would you like to sit down?"

"No, I'm all muddy." She gestured at the clean floor with a slight frown.

The thought of some mud wasn't much of a deterrent to sex in his mind, but she was a tidier person. If she needed to have her boots off, he was inclined to help. He crouched down at her feet and reached to help her unfasten the buckles that held her waterproof boots on. Her fingers tangled with his and skittered away to work at other locations. As she stepped out of the first boot, her hand landed on his shoulder while she balanced, and he liked the pressure of her palm against his muscles. Another flare of arousal warmed him and his cock thickened as the possibilities of their position tantalized. He reminded himself there was no need to rush even though his body was longing for hers. They would have all night since Brida wouldn't be back from her shift until mid-morning. What an unexpected, but completely welcome, way to conclude his day.

Teah cleared her throat and moved away from the wet puddle on the mat. She peered around the living room like she was trying to memorize the location of every piece of furniture and electronic device. He gestured toward the sofa, and with a quick little nod she scurried to it. The sofa Brida had ordered was large, soft, and perfectly suited to various copulatory arrangements. With a little sigh she sat down on the edge of a full, dark blue cushion, her feet perfectly aligned on the floor. She glanced up at him and her eyes widened slightly as he sat next to her, close enough to shift her his way, but not so near as to touch any part of her yet. He'd thought she was attractive before, but now, with the quiet house surrounding them and the evening stretching ahead, he let himself assess and appreciate her even more. Full lips, deep brown eyes, and little tumbles of curling russet hair, damp from the rain. Unusual, but very pretty.

"You're probably wondering why I'm here," she said in a rush. "I've just been thinking about this for a couple of days and knew I wouldn't be able to sleep tonight if I didn't deal with it."

Not an especially ringing endorsement of coitus, more like something she was checking off her to-do list, but he was sure he could please her. She didn't seem to need a reply because she continued.

"I've heard some rumors. Gossip. People like to talk about newcomers."

Ah, she was worried their assignation might become common knowledge. "Most of it is baseless, I'm sure."

She shook her head and again clasped her hands together. "Have you spoken with Bokum again?"

Eidan paused, drawn from his study of the shape of her mouth by her abrupt change in subject. General conversation before intimacy was certainly acceptable, especially if it put her at ease. Once they began he was sure she wouldn't be able to string a sentence together. Eleoni women were quite demanding, so he was certain his sexual abilities would overwhelm a human female. "No. Is there some story about him?"

Her hand crept his way and clutched at the sofa cushion. "Yes. He's, well, he's untrustworthy. A criminal."

Eidan nodded encouragement for her to continue. She leaned closer and lowered her voice.

"He's not happy you're here. Either of you, or Collective law for that matter. He has a lot of power in this town. A lot to lose."

"I'm aware," Eidan said, wondering how to get her back on track to intercourse. He wasn't worried about the maneuverings of a minor extortionist in this isolated place. He'd faced down contract killers, rogue bounty hunters, and armed gangs in his time as a chief investigations officer on Eleon. A small man in a muddy suit was hardly going to evade the law when Eidan moved to enforce it. "I appreciate you coming to tell me about it."

Her brows drew together. "I had to. You're in some peril and deserve to know."

Ahh, so she harbored kind feelings toward him. That would make their encounter all the more passionate. He leaned a little closer.

"There's something else," Teah said as her cheeks flushed pink. This was looking promising. "It might not be something that you're interested in anyway, so I hesitate to mention it."

She smelled sweet, of some sort of flower he'd encountered long ago and forgotten until now.

"I'm embarrassed to bring it up," she said in a quivery voice, a quick smile flitting across her mouth. He wondered if human women were as passive during a sexual encounter as rumor had it.

"I think our conversation has gone remarkably well so far," he replied with as an encouraging tone as possible.

"It's ah, about sex."

As soon as the words left her lips his whole body tensed. Any doubts he had about finding a human female arousing were firmly erased by the primal surge in his body. She gripped the seat cushion even harder, and he wondered why she wasn't holding him that tightly. Before he could suggest that course of action, she took a deep breath and continued.

"I've also heard rumors that the sex workers aren't going to accommodate you or Brida. I just wanted to tell you and save you some awkwardness. Unless you've already been there?" Her eyes were wide again, and he stared into them, waiting for her words to make some sense.

"Sex workers?"

"Yes, over at the Pleasure Spread. They're boycotting any Eleoni transactions. The men, the women, and I think the morph will refuse as well. Their union is really supportive of whatever the membership wants, and Boris can't do anything about it." She nodded quickly.

"The morph?" Eidan knew he was fumbling, but to go from the anticipation of an incoming copulation to being told sex workers wouldn't entertain his business was difficult to reconcile. He swallowed hard.

"Yes. Vonnie, the morph, is modified to have all sorts of genitalia." She gave him a little smile and

35

released her hold on the sofa before standing up. "All right, that wasn't so bad."

Wasn't so bad? Discovering she'd merely come here only to warn him about an already known threat, and that apparently humans found Eleoni unpalatable were two fairly negative outcomes.

"Are you going?"

"Of course. Unless you have some questions?"

"I thought—" He hadn't been able to suppress the sharp tone, and she picked up on it judging by her narrowed eyes. It was late, he was tired, faced with many challenges, and her sudden move to leave indicated he wasn't going to be having sex with her, or apparently anyone else on this planet for that matter. *Not* the best way to conclude his day.

Teah took a step back, her gaze trained on him. "You thought what?"

A sigh filled with frustration hissed out of his lungs. "I thought nothing."

"It's good to know my efforts to help are so appreciated." Teah sniffed. "Good night."

She'd made it to her boots by the time he realized she was fleeing, and he rose from his seat to intercept her. As he approached, her movements became more erratic as she fumbled with the muddy buckles and straps. She unbent from her crouch and stumbled back, reaching behind her for the wet slicker. Shrugging into the garment, she avoided his gaze.

"Good night," she repeated.

"You already said that."

"Do I need to say more?"

Eidan watched her as a dissatisfied ache churned inside. Yes, he wanted to say, you need to explain why you're really here, why you're running now, why you don't seem to like me but still ventured into my home in the dark of night to warn me about issues I'm fully capable of handling on my own.

"Absolutely not. I require nothing more. Good evening, Sheriff Cozad." Teah held out her hand, clearly hoping for a civilized parting. He obliged her, taking her cool hand in his and repressing the urge to hold on and pull her back over to the sofa behind them. Some companionship, even if platonic, might be what he needed to improve his outlook.

"It's raining out there."

Slipping on her coat with a snap that sent droplets flying, she nodded once. "I'm aware. I walked through it to get here."

"I thought you might want to wait until it lessened."

"This is Rusk. It never stops." Her hand on the door latch, she turned back and leveled a cool glare on him. Perversely, his body warmed up again. "Good night."

"You keep saying that. Where do you live?" Even as he spoke he was putting on his own foul weather gear, conveniently located next to the door.

She frowned and tilted her head back. "Why? I know the way."

Eidan stopped moving with his coat halfway pulled up his arms. How could explain his impulse to her when he didn't understand it himself? She was an independent adult who'd been living in the settlement for months, much more capable of finding her way in the dark than he was at this point. He'd gotten lost just that morning trying to respond to a reported burglary. As he struggled to formulate a reply, she was gone, disappearing into the dark before he could call her back.

****

The damp air cooled her overheated skin and Teah let out a sigh of relief as she walked away from the sheriff's absurdly luxurious house. She'd never seen such nice furnishings or a more pleasantly designed space. Entering such an elegant dwelling here on sloppy, backward Rusk had been a shock and likely explained how hot she'd felt while she'd been there. The rich colors, how soft the upholstery had been under her fingers as she'd perched on that sinfully comfortable sofa, everything had dazzled. She wasn't made for such things, and she'd grown more and more uncomfortable the longer she'd been there.

As she walked, pulling her feet from the mud's suction with every step, she had to admit she was also relieved to be away from Eidan. The sheriff yet again put her off balance with his staring and rumbling out questions like she was a hardened criminal he was interrogating. The sound of squelching footsteps behind her made her belly draw up and she spun around, ready to confront whoever was shadowing her. It paid to be cautious on the streets of Rusk at any time, but especially at night.

A tall figure emerged from the dark mist, and her breath stopped. Rain dripped from a wide brimmed black hat and ran in rivulets down a long wet coat. She clutched her fingers at her waist, absurdly searching for a non-existent weapon. One step closer and she recognized a grim-faced Eidan Cozad. All her pent up breath escaped in a rush, and she doubled over as her taut muscles relaxed.

There was the splashing of feet in the mud and suddenly hands were under her elbows, helping her straighten. A flush of relief and residual fear filled her with indignation.

"What are you doing out here?"

"Walking you back. Why didn't you wait?"

"Because I didn't require an escort."

"If it's so safe, why were you frightened just now?" His question was logical, which irritated her.

"You just startled me. I'm not afraid."

He compressed his lips and narrowed his eyes. All right, lying to him was probably a bad choice. Most of the people he encountered every day probably set out to deceive him, and were far more skilled at it than she was. Deciding arguing was not a smart strategy when dealing with a law enforcement official, she turned on her heel and strode away, keeping her eyes trained on the slippery ground in front of her. As she'd suspected they would, footsteps followed immediately.

A few more meters covered and she'd had all she could take. Whirling again, she nearly rammed her face into his wide chest since he'd somehow crept very close. Tightening her shoulders, she stared up into his violet eyes, nearly purple in the black of Rusk's night. The three small moons of this planet provided very little reflected light no matter where they were in the cycle.

"Why are you following me?"

"I'm not following you. I'm patrolling my jurisdiction." Even in the dark she saw something flicker in his eyes. She didn't know him well enough to guess what could be lurking inside his Eleoni mind.

"Well, go patrol somewhere else."

His full lips quirked, and a sudden spurt of irrational curiosity filled her. Was his beard scratchy or soft? "This area requires my attention."

Huffing out a breath of frustration, she walked away again, determined not to increase her pace too much and have him think she was fleeing. She reached the correct cross street and swung left, her boots hitting the raised walkway with a hollow thump. Mere seconds later

Eidan's steps clumped behind her. Frustrated and feeling ridiculous at the same time, she slowed and angled her body so she could see him.

"Are you really going to dog my steps the whole way?"

"What does dog mean?"

Reminded yet again of his alienness, Teah told herself to be more patient. "Dogs are earth carnivores. People keep them as pets and use them for work. Some dogs herd livestock by nipping at their heels, so when someone follows close behind, we say they are dogging our steps."

Nodding once, Eidan extended his stride to join her. "So these carnivores live with you? Don't they bite?"

Shaking her head, she wondered how much detail he wanted. Probably a lot, he struck her as a thorough person. "Sometimes they do, but for the most part, they see humans as their family and everyone gets along. There are even a few dogs here in Rusk. Don't you have pets on Eleon?"

Eidan shrugged as he scanned the street in front of them. "Some children keep small mammals as companions, and there are several species of reptile that are popular in certain circles."

"But you're not an animal lover?"

"I've never met a loveable animal."

Teah debated whether to mention Broose, but before she could bring up her orphaned aircuttle, the sound of raised voices caught her attention. Eidan's, too, for he turned in the direction of the sound and stilled. The disturbance, quieting now, seemed to have originated from an alley nearby.

Eidan reached out and touched her waist. The unexpected contact made her jump. "Stay here."

With a flick of his hand he activated some sort of communication device and announced his location and intention to investigate a suspicious sound. He then strode away, easing the long folds of his slicker away from his waist where she spotted a belt festooned with all sort of implements. The dark closed around her, and a tickle of unease worked its way under her skin as he disappeared into the now silent alley. From behind her she heard a scuffle and the clatter of feet running. Tension gripped her, and she spun around, creeping closer and closer to the entrance of the alley even as she scanned the gloom around her. Few lights, doors and windows sealed up against the night—this section of Rusk was residential and quiet, a far cry from the raucous activity and constant visitors of the main street that teemed with bars, gambling dens, and restaurants. Here it was deserted, and even though she delivered mail along this street in the daylight hours, the familiar structures loomed in a menacing way once the sun went down.

Another, louder sound crashed from the alley entrance, and she jumped. Two shadowy figures emerged at a stumbling run, their trajectory taking them directly into Teah's path. She tried to dodge, but they were too quick, or she was too slow. With a bone-jarring thud one of them hit her torso with a hard shoulder and she was flung into the side of the building. The wet planks of the walk did little to cushion her fall, and she sprawled, her body weight crushing her left hand at an awkward angle. For a stunned moment she lay with limbs akimbo as her chest throbbed and the bent fingers of her hand sent terrible daggers of pain up her arm.

She heard rapid footsteps splashing away as she gathered her legs under her. Damp soaked into her knees and she couldn't stop the groan welling up from her throat. Strong hands caught at her arm and around her waist, and she struggled a moment, thinking someone was going to fling her again.

"It is Eidan Cozad. I will help you rise." Without delay he'd lifted her up effortlessly. She clutched her injured hand to her aching chest and tried to catch her breath. It had all happened so quickly, she was dizzy.

"What happened?" As he spoke, he touched her wrist, trying to angle her arm out into the small pool of light provided by a tiny lantern hanging from a hook overhead.

"They knocked me down. Are you going to chase them?"

"It's not illegal to be in an alley or run from a stranger. Besides, I would never catch them at this point."

His mild answer irritated her. "Then why did you barge in there?"

"I was curious and it was my duty." He stopped looking at her hand, which was in one piece but she could already feel the fingers swelling, and frowned at her. "I'm sorry you were injured."

"It'll be all right," she lied, and he narrowed his eyes at her. Caught again.

"No, I will escort you to the medical clinic." He looked around the dark street, clearly lost.

"It's not that bad," she said as she flexed her fingers enough that the resulting pain made her wince. The muck that had soaked into her pants was now cold and clammy against her skin. So far, her mission to help the Eleoni had gone from awkward to uncomfortable.

He reached out for her waist as if he was going to capture her, and she stumbled back to avoid his unexpected gesture.

"What? I merely wish to ensure you come with me." He advanced a step with his hand out, and she batted at it with her uninjured hand. It was like trying to bend an oak branch. She backed into the side of a modular unit as he settled his fingers at her waist. They clamped down firmly, tight enough that she couldn't move. At the same moment his other hand circled her from the other side. Trapped. Futilely she pushed at him as she cradled her injured hand between them. He leaned closer and studied her with a puzzled air.

"Why are you grabbing me?"

"I'm escorting you to the clinic. Your accident was my responsibility. Why are you struggling?"

She pushed at his arms again, his nearness sparking a vulnerability she didn't like, the tiny space left between their bodies making it difficult to gain any leverage. His feet landed on either side of hers as she wriggled, and his thighs pressed close. Thick, solid thighs immobile against hers. A blast of anxiety at being restrained warred with her sudden awareness of his masculinity and her whole body quivered. His face was close to hers, and she struggled to maintain eye contact under his intent regard. It seemed she needed to do some more cross cultural training.

"You touching my body like this is uncomfortable for me."

Immediately he released his hold, and she sucked in a breath. There wasn't that much room to inhale. He hadn't stepped back, and she was still wedged up against the building. "How should I touch you?"

That was a loaded question. "You don't need to touch me. I'm going to walk home, not run away from you."

He shook his head once. "I'm sensing you wish to flee. Does my presence disturb you?"

More and more, she thought. Time for another lie. "No. It's just that people don't touch each other's waists, torsos for that matter, unless they're..."

"Unless they're what?"

The stress and confusion burning her from the inside out seemed to concentrate in her cheeks and she knew she was blushing furiously. "Unless they are in a very close relationship."

He nodded once as understanding apparently dawned. "Where would it be appropriate for me to touch you? As acquaintances?"

She accepted that he was determined to keep some sort of physical contact with her. Perhaps it was an Eleon custom. "My arm."

Without a word he stepped to the side and loosely gripped her uninjured arm above the elbow. It was close to the posture of an arresting officer leading a perpetrator to a holding cell, but less unnerving than having him nearly embrace her. "I don't like the notion of you not being examined by a trained medical professional. The first ninety minutes following an injury are vital for prompt treatment and full recovery."

He sounded like he was quoting from a manual. She was suddenly amused by his formality. "I fell and banged up my fingers. It's not like I was in a cage match at midnight."

Teah couldn't help but smile at the thought of being involved in such a fracas. Organized nighttime fights were one of the main forms of entertainment on Rusk and drew large crowds. She'd never gone, as the idea held little appeal. She was normally snug in her bed soon after dark fell. Her delivery runs began at the crack of dawn, and violence made her ill in any case. He made a dissatisfied sound under his breath and gripped her arm tighter.

"Do you engage in those?"

Teah shook her head and almost laughed. The humor of the situation was helping take her mind off the throbs that issued from her hand with every stumbling step she took. "Only every other Third-day evening."

He stopped suddenly and stared at her as she also halted. "Today is Second-day."

Now the laugh burbled out. She couldn't help herself even though it was probably not a good career move to laugh at the sheriff. "I'm joking."

His lips tightened as he regarded her. With a tiny nod like he'd discovered some interesting fact, he gestured for her to keep walking.

****

Eidan tried to hide his surprise when Teah headed for a narrow exterior staircase attached to the post office and declared she lived above her work. An attic did not seem a fitting location for a Collective representative, but as she gingerly made her way up the stairs, hampered by her injured hand, she cheerfully explained it saved on her commute time for work.

They reached the tiny landing at the top of the steps and she plugged in her security code. Eidan told himself to forget it as soon as he'd memorized it, but he doubted his brain would obey. Standing at this height gave him the opportunity to make a quick reconnaissance of Rusk's rooftops, not that he could see much in the misty gloom.

With a slight creak the door opened and she ducked inside, calling out for him to enter if he liked. Pulled along by an urge to make certain her injuries were cared for, he stepped over the raised threshold, mindful of her propensity for footwear removal. She'd already turned on a few lights, and just as he took in bare floors and blank walls a pulsating red and yellow object flew at his face. Startled by the sudden movement, he stepped back and his heels caught on the threshold. Overbalancing, he half fell against the railing of the landing even as he flung his hands up to strike at the fluttering thing that had followed him outside.

Teah shrieked and flung herself across his chest, and he automatically circled one arm around her even as he scanned the air for the return of the flying thing, whatever it was.

"Careful of your hand," he cautioned her.

"Damn Broose," she said as she stared in his face. "Did he mist you?"

Eidan could only look dumbly at her, confused by what she'd asked him, as well as impressed by her soft body atop his. If only they weren't swaddled by this absurdly abundant raingear, he'd be able to gain a much more tactile impression of her. His cock didn't care. Despite the ridiculous circumstances, it swelled and warmed, clearly ready to retire for the evening to Teah's bed.

"Did he…" Teah frowned hand swept her fingertips across his cheeks and the bridge of his nose. Her touch was light but still made his skin prickle with awareness. "No, thank goodness. It's such a mess to clean up."

She struggled to her feet and held out a hand to help him up. He took it and rose, thankful the railing behind him had held. He could have broken his back if he'd fallen to the ground. Teah tugged him back inside her small apartment, and he willingly followed, not too concerned with whatever the red and orange thing had been since she was not behaving in a frightened manner.

Once they were back indoors, she shut the door quickly and continued her inspection of him. The light was better, so he took the opportunity to check her hand. He'd been worried one of her fingers might have been broken or dislocated, but they all seemed intact, if bruised and swollen. Teah rubbed her palms across his chest and he shrugged out of his slicker, willing for her to get closer to him but was disappointed when she gathered up the garment and hung it on a peg by the door. She placed her own next to it, then stepped out of her boots. He remembered to remove his own, and as he bent down to unfasten the buckles, he hoped they both might continue to shed articles of clothing.

As he rose from his crouch, her heard a faint hissing gasp and caught reddish movement from the corner of his eye. The thing was in the air again. Drawing up to his full height, he pivoted to face it, ready to strike if need be. In a flash, Teah stood in front of him, facing the swooping object, and he again grabbed her, trying to move her from harm's way. She gripped his arm with her free hand and made crooning noises at the thing.

Now that he could see it better, he realized it was some sort of animal, smooth skinned and nebulous. Long tendrils fell from a conical body about thirty centimeters long as it hovered nearby. Two large black eyes were locked upon them. The surface of the creature pulsed red, orange, and all shades of yellow as it hovered.

"Now, Broose, don't be jealous. Sheriff Cozad isn't going to take you away from me," Teah told the thing, and it extended a tendril her way. Teah tried to stay in front of him as a shield even as he attempted to ease her behind him and away from the hovering animal. Eidan also tried not to be distracted by how nicely her buttocks curved against his hips as friction grew between them. He belatedly realized she could probably feel his cock hardening at the warm press of her body. The creature, Broose, moved closer, and Eidan would have sworn the black eyes fixed on him with extreme suspicion. It was now close enough for the tentacles to touch her hair, and she sang a few nonsense words at it as it lifted a braid from her head and fondled it.

"That's it. See? He's a nice man," she said in a singsong way, and Broose shaded from vibrant red to a soft pinkish violet. "There. Now you're calm."

Teah pushed on his arm, and he reluctantly released her. Broose floated behind her head, one malevolent inky eye glaring at Eidan. She cupped her uninjured hand around the damaged one. "Were you hurt in that fall? I'm sorry he startled you. He's usually asleep at this hour. I thought we'd be able to sneak in and avoid his usual threat displays."

Eidan assured her he was fine while he kept a wary eye on the creature. "Will it attack again?"

"Not unless he's startled."

Satisfied they weren't under immediate threat from the airborne animal, Eidan turned his attention to Teah. "Do you have a first aid kit? I'd like to examine your hand. I can tell you're in pain by the way you're shielding it."

"It's not—" Her mouth closed when he shook his head. "You're right. It hurts."

A few steps brought them to a well-lit, if miniscule, kitchen area, and she opened a nearly bare cabinet to retrieve a standard first aid kit. He took charge of it and quickly applied a disposable scanner to her hand. As the thin membrane melded to her skin to evaluate tissue damage he looked her over for other injuries. Her trousers were spattered with mud, but when he inquired after further problems she shook her head, her floating companion echoing the movement. With a gentle beep, the scanner indicated all necessary data had been collected, and he bent to read the results. Soft tissue damage only, with the recommended treatment of cold therapy and anti-inflammatory. Without asking her permission, since he knew she'd simply deny him, Eidan ran warm water and eased her hand under the stream, washing away the traces of mud with some soap conveniently located nearby. She only put up a token resistance, and he felt her body relax somewhat as he took it upon himself to cleanse her other hand. A wave of purple caught his peripheral vision as Teah disentangled her fingers from his and dried them on a towel.

"What is a broose?"

"His name is Broose," Teah said as he cracked open the analgesic ointment from the packet and rubbed it along the bases of her fingers. The scan had indicated those joints were the more severely traumatized. "He's an aircuttle. Or what I call an aircuttle. The scientists call them Morgela donfritis, but most people around here call them wet sacks."

Her voice trembled a bit and he wondered if he'd hurt her, so he lightened his touch as he stroked the pain reliever along her fingers. "How did he come to live with you?"

She sighed, and he peered into her deep brown eyes as she blinked. Broose eased even closer to her and clasped a few more strands of her hair with his waving violet tentacles. His big black eyes tracked Eidan for a moment, then flickered down to the woman below him.

"I was on a delivery run, about a month after arriving here and came across a lot of dead cuttles scattered across the trail. Someone had shot them. They live in groups and aren't habituated to fear humans yet, so sometimes people use them for target practice." She hitched in a breath and hunched her shoulders. "I picked up the bodies to bury them, and by the time I was nearly done, I found Broose. He was just a baby, clinging to a piece of grasswood. He'd turned black with the trauma, maybe grief. I don't know."

She reached up with her free hand and stroked the side of the creature's body. Broose pulsed pink and trailed a few tendrils around her wrist. The animal made that faint hissing puff again. Eidan cleared his throat, unsure how to comfort her. "There are several statutes against animal cruelty in the Collective mandate. Would you say such activities are common?"

Teah sniffed and leaned closer to inspect her hand, flexing the fingers slightly against his palm. "I hate to say it, but more often than I would have thought. There's always a few cruel people, but something about being way out here, so isolated, seems to bring out bad behavior in lots of folks."

She stiffened and looked up at him, her face close to his as she bit her lip. "Goodness, I shouldn't have said that. Not all people are like that. Not everyone in Rusk is bad."

"I know."

Her wry smile captured his attention, and he realized he was interested in her opinions, not just her physical charms. It was an unexpected development.

****

The water was still running. Teah knew she should turn it off, should change the topic of conversation, should encourage Broose back to his favorite perch, and most of all should take her hand from Sheriff Cozad's, but she couldn't move. She was stalled, standing there in her tiny kitchen as she relived how sad she'd felt when she'd cleaned up the destroyed remnants of Broose's family. She was probably wrong to assert that humans were good considering all the depraved things she'd seen and heard about since arriving on Rusk. Her own upbringing hadn't been the most nurturing, and her future had seemed grim until she'd scored well on the Collective civil service exam and the possibility of a new life with steady pay and benefits had been granted. She'd thought she was tough until she'd landed on Rusk.

The sheriff watched her with those lavender eyes, and she wanted to stare into them. The color was so fascinating, the little hints of his thoughts kept her looking at him. He was a different species, a powerful man new to this ramshackle community, but at this moment she could pretend he was simply a kind friend helping her. Tomorrow she'd again take on the worry that he and his sister were in peril from the criminals who wandered freely in Rusk. Tonight was just a quiet conversation in the safety of her little home.

"How is your hand?" His rumbling question snapped her out of her musings, and she glanced down to see him again stroking her fingers with the lightest of touches. Before, when he'd been washing and applying the pain reliever, her hand had ached, but now there was only a slight tug of soreness as she flexed her fingers.

"Better."

"Apply a cold compress next."

"You're going?" Teah pressed her lips together, confused by her question. Of course he was leaving. She hadn't even wanted him to come here when she'd left his house. Somehow over the course of the last hour she'd gone from wanting to get far away from him, to hoping he'd linger and talk. Perhaps it was due to the close calls they'd recently shared.

"It's not appropriate for me to stay longer."

Ah, gossip. It seemed he'd taken her warning to heart. "Of course. Thank you for your help."

"Thank you for your earlier advice." Was that a hint of a smile on his lips? The short beard covering his chin and framing his mouth helped disguise his facial expressions, and she wondered if that was why he'd grown out his facial hair. Or perhaps that was the fashion for vital men on Eleon. It was very masculine-looking. Was he equally hirsute elsewhere? A flush of heat prickled along her skin at that thought, and she remembered how shivery she'd felt when he'd wrapped her up tight to his body as he'd thought to shield her from Broose's nonexistent threat. His arms had been as hard as forged titanite and the torso pressed to her back had been solid muscle.

With a little sigh, he released her hands. In a few efficient movements he'd turned off the water, packed away the first aid kit, and hung up the towel. Broose drifted the sheriff's way and puffed out his mantle in a flutter of rose red, but Teah could tell the little animal's heart wasn't in it. They were all tired.

"So he's your pet?" Eidan asked as he peered at the aircuttle turning in a slow circle around the ceiling light fixture.

"Not really. I'm just his temporary caretaker, until he decides to return to the forest."

He considered her for a moment, then inclined his head in a courtly gesture and moved to the door. It only took him a few steps, as her room was small. Broose stayed by the kitchen light fixture, his revolutions slowing as he relaxed towards sleep. She'd have to remember to guide him over to his favorite perch by the window before she went to bed.

Suddenly feeling awkward about having a strange man in her home, she paused with her hand on the doorframe, unsure what sort of parting gesture Eleoni preferred.

"We had a few adventures tonight," she said, tickles of uncertainty fluttering in her belly. He probably thought she was a lunatic wandering around at night and keeping a strange creature in her home. "Lots of mishaps and bad luck. Making bad impressions."

He was silent as he put on his foul weather gear. Once he was covered up and waterproof again, he gave her a cool glance. "I regret any distress I caused you or your pet."

Teah wondered what she'd said that would have dissipated that inkling of camaraderie she'd thought she'd sensed between them. Before she could think of what to say to make it right, he was out the door and thumping down the steps.

Chapter Three

Brida was irritating. His sister tapped the edge of one of her throwing dagger's scabbards on the heel of her boot and the clicking sound echoed in the silent security station, the noise sounding completely out of proportion. Eidan had been on edge all morning after a night of tattered dreams and interrupted sleep. As he went through the prior shift's report before taking command from Brida, he had to suppress both a yawn and a snapped command that she cease and desist her pointless racket before he relieved her of her weapon. Another series of clicks sent him over the edge.

"Stop doing that."

"What?" Her tone was all older sister pretending innocence, and contained not a trace of subordinate officer. Granted, she'd been up all night and was anxious to head home for sleep once he'd relieved her, but protocol mattered, even out here in the far reaches of space. Perhaps it mattered even more here. He should be more patient with her, considering how fragile she had to be feeling as her body chemistry returned to normal, but it seemed he didn't have the will at the moment.

Before he could remonstrate further, the door opened and he looked up to see two large and tattered-looking human males stride in. Grimy clothes draped over their thick bodies, and both peered around the office and holding cells beyond with slight sneers. One had a broken front tooth, and the other sported a sparse mustache.

"Can we help you?" Brida spoke up as she casually slid her dagger back into her boot top. Eidan could read her alertness increase at the unexpected visitation.

"Doubt it, kitty cat." Mustache drawled, barely cutting his eyes at her. Both men's focus rested squarely on Eidan. Brida smiled. "We need to deal with this tom here. Your brother, right?"

"That's right," his sister said, ostentatiously propping her boots up on the edge of the desk as if she hadn't a care in the world. The two humans couldn't see from their position, but she had her shock gun angled their way, hidden by the edge of the piece of furniture.

"Keeping it in the family." Toothless smirked as he reached into one of his layers of jacket. Brida tensed, and Eidan braced his feet, ready to move quickly if need be. The grimy man pulled out a smallish paper-covered cube and tossed it on the desk in front of Eidan. Both humans looked at him with equal expressions of expectation.

"What's this?" Eidan kept his voice level, even though he wondered if there was some sort of explosive or biological agent hidden within.

"Your consideration." Mustache straightened his clothes like he was readying for a gritty formal ball.

"Consideration of what?"

"It's the usual take." Toothless shuffled his feet, clearly ready to leave. "Just making the rounds. Usually it's fifty-fifty split with the deputies." He gestured his head at Brida, and she grinned like he was the most charming conversationalist she'd ever encountered.

So this was the first attempt at a payoff. The only question was who was behind it, Bokum or some player he hadn't met yet. Eidan pulled a small threader prod from his belt and poked at the package, noticing the two men puffing up their chests as they recognized the weapon. So they were confident in their ability to beat him, and likely thought Brida was no threat. He wasn't willing to educate them yet.

"Who sent this?"

"The main man."

"Pardon me, I'm new here. Who exactly is the main man?"

Toothless and Mustache glanced at each other, comically pitying looks on their faces. If humans expressed that emotion in a similar fashion of eye rolling and tiny head shakes. "Bokum. You met him before."

Eidan nodded. He had been expecting this, but was a bit disappointed another man fancying himself the power behind the throne hadn't made contact yet. Perhaps Bokum truly was the main player in Rusk. In any case, it was time to establish some boundaries with his human constituency.

Before he could reply, the door behind the hulking men swung open, whoever opened it too short to be seen. The two men rocked on their feet as a soft, familiar voice asked for pardon and as they stepped aside, Teah emerged. She was dressed in full postal regalia with every pleat knife-sharp and all buttons gleaming. Her soft hair was tucked up under a regulation cap, and she blinked when she saw him. Unease wound through his nerves as he watched her edge her way between the two toughs, apparently unaware she was brushing against criminals. Eidan didn't like that at all. She approached the desk, her cart bumping along behind her, and nodded to Brida who kept her gaze fixed on the men.

"Hello, Sheriff, Deputy," Teah said as she rummaged inside a pouch attached to the cart's frame. She was bent over and didn't seem to notice that her carrier bumped first into Mustache's leg, then Toothless's. Both men grimaced and stepped further away from her. She emerged with a small resin shipping box and handed it over with a smile to Brida. "Sorry, Sheriff, nothing for you today."

"But I have something for you," Eidan declared, as he suddenly made a decision. He scrambled in the desk for some sort of writing implement, but came up empty handed. "Can you produce a shipping label?"

Teah nodded and drew closer, pulling her cart along with her like she was afraid the two men would rummage through it when her back was turned. Mustache and Toothless, for their part, frowned, apparently unhappy with this mundane interruption to their attempted bribery.

Eidan gestured at the package of money lying on the desk, and Teah took it up with a dubious look at the slipshod packaging. "Not a very nice wrapping. This won't hold for long."

"It doesn't have to. I want you to deliver it to Bokum. He's nearby, isn't he?"

Teah's eyes widened, and she pressed her soft mouth into a line. "Yes, he's just a couple of streets away. I know the address." She cut her eyes to either side, probably realizing who the men behind her worked for, and then unbuttoned her tunic. Eidan was distracted from his professional crisis by her movements, and reminded himself she'd made it clear she wasn't interested in him, between bad impressions and the apparent shared human revulsion for Eleoni. No need to track her fingers as they plucked at the fasteners, no need to strain to hear the faint shush of fabric as she adjusted her clothing. She pulled her glove scanner from a pocket and expertly slid it on. With a few practiced moves she'd generated a tiny bar code and affixed it to the payoff. "That'll be fourteen pips."

Right, he had to pay for the service. He undid a few buttons of his own tunic and reached inside in a futile search for money. One of Teah's eyebrows crept up as he came up empty-handed. The irony of being without funds after rejecting a bribe was not lost on him. "Brida, do you have any money?"

"Yes, sir," she answered with alacrity, no longer behaving as a teasing older sister, but now clearly wanting to establish his command in front of Bokum's lackeys. It wouldn't go amiss if he found a way to increase that perception with the citizens of Rusk. Brida quickly handed over the required amount to Teah, and she eased the bundle into the recesses of her pouch. As she maneuvered her little cart around, bumping the shins of his unwanted visitors yet again, she shot him a quick glance he couldn't interpret. With requests for the two men to excuse her, she moved toward the door. Mustache shot out his arm and blocked her exit by pressing against the doorframe. Before Teah had even come to a halt, Eidan was up from his chair and around the desk, his nerves firing with the sudden urge to crush the other man's windpipe.

"Let her pass," he growled, his irritation with their petty graft now morphing into a simmering anger.

"You can't interfere with the progress of a postal officer in the conduct of her duties. Under article seven section forty-two of the new Collective legal code, you could face up to five years in prison and a forty-five million pip fine." Teah spoke up in an aggrieved tone. Eidan didn't know if he wanted to compliment her on her regulation quoting or pick her up and lift her out of harm's way. Instead, he crowded close to Mustache, glaring at him, even as he tried to position his body between the rancid man and the postal officer. Teah tugged at her cart and frowned.

"The prospect of five years on Ogon is enough to curdle my belly," Brida spoke up, as she, too, rose from her seat. His sister sent him a quick, inquiring look and for a half second, Eidan realized his aggressive move was out of character, but he was still too angry to ease back to a more controlled posture.

Mustache glanced among all three uniformed Collective service personnel and swallowed loudly. His compatriot swelled his chest a bit like he was ready to join in a potential thumping, but as soon as Mustache dropped his arm and took a half a step back, he sighed and relaxed his shoulders.

"No stress, little soldier, I just happen to know what's in that package and got a little concerned."

Teah sucked in a deep breath. "I'm a well-trained, bonded professional. That package has the guarantee of the entire Collective postal service behind its proper delivery, with insurance values of up to twenty-five million pips." She paused and pushed the door open. "And another thing, I'm not a soldier."

Belying her words, she marched out into the rain with a ramrod straight posture that would have blended admirably with the Collective Marine honor guard. Only the erratic, squeaking progress of her delivery cart following her lessened the impact of her exit.

Eidan drew back from the door, fighting his impulse to follow along and see how Teah handled her other interactions with the denizens of Rusk.

"Bokum's not going to be pleased about this," Toothless pronounced with a slight, whistling lisp. "Your time here just got unpleasant."

"Was that a threat?" Brida spoke up sharply, and both human men again barely glanced at her.

"Come on, Bob. Seems like this new sheriff has plenty of women set to fight in his place." Mustache tried on a superior smirk. Eidan simply walked back to his desk, uninterested in legitimizing their attempts to belittle him and women in the same breath. There would be a reckoning soon enough. The men shambled out the door and ostentatiously slammed it shut.

Brida walked to the window to spy on the minions' progress down the walk. "So, that was interesting."

"It came sooner than I expected." Eidan allowed as he shifted a few things on his desk top. He wondered how Teah was feeling. He suddenly regretted involving her in the minor fracas. "But we both knew the offer was bound to happen. At this point we need to consolidate our position and gather information. Confrontation and prosecution later."

Brida scoffed. "Which would explain why you were so snarly with them."

Eidan didn't care to examine why he'd rushed them. Showing his temper was a bad move in this game he was playing with Bokum. A serious game, with the highest of stakes.

"You want me to follow them?" His sister craned her neck as she peered out the window, anxious to hunt. "We don't have monitors set up everywhere yet."

"I thought you wanted to get some sleep."

She wrinkled her nose. "Just until they go to ground. Then I'll head home."

Eidan waved her on. It was good to see her enthusiastic once again. Perhaps her meld was fading already.

****

"I can't believe you're making me do this," Teah said, dragging her feet as she edged past several large Kotze. "See, it's too crowded. There aren't any seats now, so we might as well go. Come over to the post office and help me clear out the long term storage bunker."

Dorian gave her the exasperated look she deserved for that suggestion. They were at a warehouse, nearly empty of coral balls after the latest shipments out, but filled to capacity by human and Kotze spectators. They were here to watch the fights, a weekly occurrence overseen by various purveyors of gambling on Rusk, with Bokum taking his cut off the top. Clusters of people gathered around bookies scattered around the room, each one a careful distance from the other. Teah took a breath and didn't try very hard to look for any unoccupied seats. A mismatched array of cast-off chairs and temporary benches constructed of ply resin and shipping crates were mostly filled, the inhabitants noisily discussing the upcoming matches and replaying decisive moves from prior battles. Dorian grabbed her sleeve and pulled her closer to the fighting ring which was a square several meters in size, defined by four enormous bladders of water linked by lines of high tensile strap downs.

He quickly took a seat only a meter away from the barrier and tried to drag Teah down with him, but she resisted. Why had she ever made that stupid bet with him? She knew better than to make a wager with a professional gambler, no matter how much of a sure thing she'd thought it was.

"Come on, sit while there's still a space. Are you sure you don't want to make a bet?" Dorian asked with an excited lilt to his voice. He'd placed his wagers earlier in the day and so had no interest in joining one of the groups still making decisions. "Two fights. That was our deal. Maybe you'll get lucky and they'll be quick knockouts."

Teah grimaced and lowered herself to a seat on the narrow board. It seemed she was no longer going to be able to avoid Rusk's favorite spectator sport. She could handle a couple of fights. The combatants would most likely swing and miss a lot of the time because why would anyone actually want to break every bone in his hand by hammering away at someone else's thick skull?

"You look like you're facing the executioner." Dorian smirked. "It's not like you're going in the ring. Although we might be splashed by some sweat or blood."

Teah swallowed down a wave of nauseating nerves. As if there was some cue she'd missed, the noise level in the room peaked, and there was a sudden press of bodies around her as people sought their places around the ring. A large light fixture was centered directly over it, so there would be no way any of the pummeling would be hidden in shadow. Suddenly hemmed in on all sides, she knew she was trapped for the duration.

"It's mean of you to make me do this. You know I'm squeamish."

Dorian smirked. "You *think* you're squeamish. How do you know if you've never watched? Plus, putting in an appearance here gives you some credibility."

"Credibility with who? For what?" Teah shook her head. Granted, she usually came across as prim, thanks to her sheltered upbringing and determination to represent herself well, but not going to bare knuckle fights in her spare time could hardly been seen as some sort of weakness. Surely others in Rusk avoided this venue. She was diverted from her introspection when a gravelly voice rumbled out over some sort of public address system. A large grey-haired woman wearing a baggy red jumpsuit awkwardly ducked under one of the straps and stood at the center of the ring. As she held her hands up, the crowd's noise level went from raucous chatter to loud murmuring.

"It's time to start. All books are closed." The throng clapped and howled, and Teah repressed a shiver of anxiety. She could almost feel the spectators' lust for violence crawl across her skin. Again she swallowed, pushing down the knot of nerves that was jumping in her throat.

"First up is a special match. We have a new fighter who's taking on one of our favorites. Welcome back Hedak Copter," the woman called out, and there was a flurry of movement in one corner of the building. A tall, muscular man wearing only trousers, heavy boots, and thick gloves strode out past spectators who cheered and clapped him on the back. Copter's pale blue eyes didn't waver from the ring, and he entered it with the ease of long practice. Menace seemed to drip from his pores and mingle with the sweat covering the bulging muscles of his chest, back, and arms. He shook his shoulders and scanned the crowd with a lowered brow.

"And the challenger is freshly arrived from our new leaders." The woman flung out her hand, and Teah went cold with foreboding. "Sheriff Eidan Cozad, here to show us why Eleon has the right to boss us around."

The mob erupted with jeering catcalls. Teah looked around quickly, wondering where Eidan might be and if he'd survive his passage through this press of people who sounded as if they'd like to beat him before he even got to Copter. A flutter of movement in the crowd revealed an auburn head, hair carefully tied up in knotted braids. It was the sheriff, moving slowly past people who made no effort to shift and allow his passage. Teah looked for his sister but didn't spot her. Brida was probably working, although it would make sense for her to be at the fights considering at least half of Rusk's population was crowded in this room. Eidan reached the edge of the fighting circle opposite her and bent under the lines, keeping his gaze on his opponent as the people in the seats howled, some yelling crude references to *pussies*.

"Why do they keep shouting that cat stuff?" Teah asked Dorian as she gripped the hard edge of the resin board that served as her seat. It was either hold on or run away. Her friend quirked an eyebrow.

"You've heard the rumors, right? That they have feline DNA and that's why their eyes are so weird. Plus people are saying they have extra, ah, fur on their bodies."

"This in addition to the stripes? How would anyone even know?" Teah blinked. What a bizarre idea. She looked at Eidan with new interest. He wasn't half-bared like Copter, but instead wore a formfitting exercise shirt that clung to broad shoulders and thick arms. The rest of him was covered in trim pants and boots, and his hands were encased in padded gloves. What she could see looked eminently humanoid.

Some dunce in the crowd began to meow, and soon it seemed most humans in attendance were echoing the call. The Kotze glanced around with some confusion. Clearly this insult was human-centric. None of the hubbub appeared to make an impact on Eidan. He merely stood in place and watched Copter without pause. The human fighter shifted on his feet and made jabbing feints at his opponent, but Eidan didn't flinch.

The older woman raised her hands and pointed to water bladders in opposite corners, and both Eidan and Copter stalked away from each other. The human raised his arms to encourage the crowd and they roared out epithets and instructions for him to destroy the new sheriff. No one called out for Eidan, and Teah bit her lip, so much tension filling her that her shoulders and back went rigid.

The woman in the ring called out a series of rules that made little sense to Teah, mostly involving how high legs could be raised and what parts of the foot could be used. Both men began to bounce on the balls of their feet, their readiness to come to blows apparent in the way they cocked their arms and rolled their shoulders.

She'd thought the noise of the crowd would still before the fight began, to build drama, but instead, there was an increasing din that rose into a cacophony to vibrate against her skin. In a whirl of motion, Copter leaped at Eidan. She didn't see what happened next because a large miner sitting in front of Teah jumped to her feet and blocked the view. Against her will, Teah leaned to the side to catch a glimpse of Eidan skipping back as the human fighter rushed past and bounced off one of the bladders. Copter wheeled quickly and swung at Eidan, making contact three times in quick succession. The spectators screamed delight, and Teah winced. The Eleoni absorbed the blows without seeming to notice, his violet eyes slightly narrowed as he bobbed out of the reach of Copter. The Kotze moved to the left, her bulk again blocking Teah's view. Before she realized it, she was leaning into Dorian, compelled to see what was happening between the combatants.

The human was marching towards Eidan, his clenched fists brought up in front of his face. He threw out another quick series of punches that the Eleoni dodged, and then Copter levered an enormous kick at Eidan's midsection. The crowd didn't even have time to gasp before Eidan blocked it with one arm, and then with a quick twist lifted his opponent's leg high enough to tip the man over on his back. Copter fell with a bone-fracturing crash. Teah couldn't understand how the sheriff had moved so quickly and judged the angles and force required so accurately.

Cries of disbelief rang out amongst the general primal roar of the people around her, and sweat prickled along Teah's skin. She couldn't quite catch her breath.

Eidan skipped back and waited for Copter to rise, much to the dismay of some surrounding her. Cries disparaging the sheriff's courage and killer instinct rang out, but the Eleoni didn't waver in his focus on the other man struggling to his feet. The human fighter bellowed, the veins on his sweaty forehead distending as he hurled insult after insult at Eidan. With a sudden roar, Copter launched himself at the sheriff, in an unexpected blur of speed. Teah sucked in a fearful breath, sure she would see Eidan toppled and injured. The men met in the middle of the ring, muscled arms jerking as they landed blow after blow on each other's bodies. The spectators cheered with blood lust, and Teah reeled, too dizzy from the sudden heat filling her body. Perhaps it was the closeness of the crowd, or the aggressive energy permeating the air, but she found herself gasping and shaking. Her spine tingled, and her legs quivered

Copter landed a few punches against Eidan's belly along with one sickening blow to his nose while the sheriff delivered staccato-like hits to every part of the human's face. Copter's head snapped back with every strike and his gloved hands sagged down.

With an audible grunt, Eidan brought his knee up into Copter's unprotected midsection, causing his enemy to fold over and drop to the floor. Teah leapt to her feet, impatient with the Kotze woman's continuous blocking of her field of vision. Eidan circled the downed man with a bland expression. The spectators' cheers ebbed into scattered shouts of inquiry as the woman in the red jumpsuit clambered into the ring and stared down at the twitching human.

"The match goes to the sheriff," she declared in a disbelieving tone, and the audience quieted. Teah glimpsed a few shocked faces in the crowd, but had to admit she was really looking at Eidan. He wasn't even breathing hard, but instead stood with one hand outstretched, waiting to assist the fallen man. Copter struggled to his feet and lurched away, ignoring the Eleoni as he staggered against the ropes, a few of his supporters coming forward to wipe at the blood streaming from his face and offer him water. No one approached Eidan, and the breath caught in a painful knot in Teah's chest.

Almost as if he knew she was there, Eidan found her in the crowd. His expression didn't change, but he did narrow his eyes. Hot and cold pulses jangled through her nerves, and she knew she'd had enough, that she couldn't endure any more. The noise, the press of bodies, the violence she'd just witnessed, it was all too much.

"Teah, what's going on?" Dorian stood at her side as she shook her head.

"I renege," she managed to blurt out. "I'm going."

Before he could say more, she was stumbling past the other people in her row, tripping on booted feet, brushing up against hard elbows and knees, all to reach the vaguely defined aisle. Once she found a passage she fled up it, desperate to reach the warehouse's wide-flung doors. She rushed out onto an oil-slicked loading dock and paused to orient herself to find the most direct path to her safe little home, far from the sound of fists striking flesh.

****

As soon as he spotted Teah's pale face in the crowd, Eidan froze. The bolt of awareness that shot between them was unmistakable. The compulsion to talk with her overrode all his half-formed plans on what he would do after his victory.

She stared at him, her dark eyes wide with some deep emotion Eidan needed to understand. Her soft mouth moved as she replied to some question put to her by the thin man at her side, and then she bolted off, stumbling past burly Kotze and disgruntled, grimacing humans as she fled the building.

Without much thought for protocol, which seemed in short supply in this decidedly informal venue, Eidan leaped the ropes defining the fighting space, and rushed after her. He ignored the jeers and men who deliberately stood in his way. The level of defiance and aggression directed toward him was much reduced, as had been his goal when undertaking this fight. With a gain in grudging respect from some quarters, he felt he could pursue the next item requiring his attention, namely discovering why Teah was at the fight when she'd declared such activities were not to her taste. Had she heard he was appearing and her curiosity had overcome her?

He was still mulling this over as he reached the door and paused to glance around the nearly deserted street. A flutter of movement caught his eye, and he trotted out into the mist, hoping it was her. Within a few strides he'd verified she was ahead, her stature and posture as familiar to him as if he'd known her for years. He caught up with her as they reached the scant shelter of a leaky overhang and as he reached for her elbow she jumped and spun around to face him. He'd startled her again.

Teah shuddered out a shaky breath and pressed her lips together. "You're getting wet."

Eidan hadn't even noticed the cold rain trickling down his back. He edged closer to her, away from the stream of water falling past the roof sheltering them. Her gaze searched his face, and he wondered what she was looking for. All the adrenaline from the fight and pride from his victory still coursed through his veins, making it impossible for him to divert his desire to be close to her.

"Are you all right? Did he hurt you?" She inspected his face and reached out to his cheek, her fingers hovering over the bruise he could feel swelling under the skin. Her lip trembled. "You're hurt. When I saw him hit you I just went … numb."

The glitter of impending tears filled her eyes, and without considering inappropriate touching, he reached for her. She held her arms and shoulders stiffly as he gathered her up, but with a shuddering breath against his neck, she melted into him for a blissful moment. He ordered himself to consider this as nothing more significant than the comfort he'd give anyone at a low moment. His cock flagrantly disobeyed his command as it swelled with delight at the closeness of her body. It seemed he was going to have to come to terms with the idea of cross-species wooing very soon, because not making the effort to seduce Teah was something he knew he'd regret.

Her hands slid along his chest and arms in a very stimulating way, but he realized she was merely looking for injuries when she drew back and frowned. "Are you really all right? He struck you so hard I could almost feel it in the stands."

He assured her he was undamaged, anxious that she not see him as a breakable thing. The human fighter had power but lacked finesse and patience, both of which were essential in any battle. She lowered her brows and stared at his chest, almost as if she were contemplating removing his shirt. That would be acceptable, although a dirty alley was not his preferred venue for intimate encounters, especially with a woman as lustrous as Teah.

His curiosity was like a living creature circling and stretching, ready to pounce. "Why were you there? You told me you didn't go to the fights."

"I don't. But I did." Her brow creased as she considered this dichotomy. "I lost a bet."

Her unexpected answer made him smile. Even though he hadn't spent much time with Teah, far less than he wished, truth be told, she didn't seem the sort of person to indulge in gambling. Unlike himself. To his disappointment, she took a step away, gaining a slight bit of distance from him. He longed to pull her back.

"And the penalty was attending this fight?" So much for her hearing about his impromptu effort to establish his formidability with the more nefarious denizens of Rusk, and being overcome with a lustful need to watch him demonstrate his virility.

She nodded and sighed. "My friend Dorian wanted to go and made the wager with me. I should know better than to gamble with a professional, but I was sure I'd win."

Her sad little admission intrigued him. "What was the bet?"

"Knitting."

"I don't understand." Eidan rapidly tried to review the short course of human culture study he'd completed, but this term was unfamiliar.

Teah drew her hands up and cupped her elbows as she tucked her arms around her body. Perhaps she was cold. It was a damp evening. Eidan moved closer to her.

"We knit. It's when you use needles and yarn to construct a textile. Like a sweater or scarf." She must have read his continued mystification because she held out her fingers in a peculiar, bent fashion. "We like to do that in the evening, before he starts his shift at the Last Chance and after I close up the office. We were chatting last night and he was teasing me, so to quiet him I challenged him to a purling competition. I thought I would win since he's usually so much slower, but he beat me."

Teah shook her head, apparently displeased with herself for being duped. Again, curiosity overwhelmed him. "Dorian is your partner?"

She chuckled and shook her head. "Of course not."

Eidan was puzzled yet again. Teah was beautiful and charming, so of course a man would wish to have a relationship with her. It seemed Teah found the idea ridiculous. Did she prefer women? He was going to have to review his old human relations manual very soon. Perhaps there was a section on sexual mores he'd missed.

"So that's my pathetic reason for being there. I made a bet with a professional gambler over something pointless like a hand craft, and then I was so shocked by what was happening to you I lost it and fled the scene."

A rueful grin crossed her lips.

"You'll know better next time." Eidan considered her. She seemed much calmer than she had immediately after he'd found her and it was likely she'd soon want to continue her journey home. What could he do to prolong this encounter?

****

Teah tried to keep from smiling at Eidan, but her mouth kept betraying her. She'd swung from being overwhelmed by distress at the climax of his fight to soaking up the comfort of his gentle reassurances, to amusement now. It was confusing. Equally confusing were the warm tickles of excitement jolting around her body. She *liked* talking to him, liked how easy it was, liked how she wanted to hear what he thought, wanted to answer his questions. Granted he was handsome for an Eleoni, no, handsome for a man, but it was the obvious intelligence and interest lighting in those mesmerizing violet eyes that riveted her.

She suddenly wished he was touching her again. Why had she shrugged out of his embrace?

"Did the fight add to your bad impression of me?"

His sudden question startled her, and she shook her head rapidly. "I don't have a bad impression of you. Why would you think that?"

"You said so, the other night."

"I meant me. I fell down like a clumsy fool, my aircuttle attacked you…" She didn't mention all the other things she was embarrassed by, like thinking he needed to know about the ban the sex workers had imposed. Why she'd thought that was appropriate she had no idea, now.

His eyes narrowed and seemed to darken from violet to mauve. He stepped closer, and she was again aware of his body overwhelming hers. Rationally, she knew he wasn't that much larger than she was, but somehow his solid build and confidence made him seem like a giant.

"So what is your impression of me, if it isn't bad, that is?"

"Oh, I…" Teah couldn't stop her stammer, completely off track as Eidan ran his fingertips along her arm. That's right, she'd given him permission to touch her there, but that didn't explain why her skin was prickling like she'd received an electric shock. "You ask a lot of questions."

Her obvious stall for time made him smile. "I'm curious. Part of my work here involves learning more about humans. How they think, their customs and traditions…"

Now his fingertips were tracing along her shoulder. She could barely feel the pressure through her insulated jacket, but she knew they were there nonetheless. "I thought you were here to put people in jail."

"Only the bad ones." He was so close now she could feel the warmth of his body, his eyes never leaving hers as his thumb slid along her jaw. She jumped and tilted her chin up instinctively. "I'm sure you aren't bad, Teah. I'd hazard a guess that you're very good."

Was that the first time he'd said her name? She couldn't be sure, but his deep voice was rumbling in a near purr that vibrated in her bones. "Oh, I don't know. I have my flaws."

It was pure bravado, of course, but she needed to say something to counteract the unsettled feeling circling around her belly like fluttering aircuttle.

He smiled, even white teeth flashing from the shadow of his beard. "Such as? Do you forget to recycle your trash? Delay turning in your delivery reports?"

Teah's mouth fell open. He was mocking her. It was almost irritating enough to make her not notice he was still running his fingers along her skin, and that he was close enough now his chest was almost touching hers. "I've been bad before."

"Should I run you in? Pull up your priors and check for outstanding warrants? Are you a danger to my person?"

Her temper flared. People always assumed she was so boring and responsible, just because she kept things clean and tidy and did her work well. Apparently even another species was perpetuating this misapprehension about her personality. A burst of inspiration filled her and she acted, making her move before her courage failed her.

****

Eidan had been enjoying himself immensely. Watching Teah's outrage grow as her eyes sparkled and

73

her cheeks flushed, had made him forget all about the bruises forming on his torso and the chill rain surrounding them with grim humidity. He hadn't teased a pretty woman in far too long.

He'd taken advantage of her distraction and moved close to her, his body urging him to stay near, be as tactile as possible because everywhere he touched made him want more. She didn't seem to be searching for an escape as she had upon their earlier acquaintance, but that might be because she was so aggravated. She frowned, and he braced himself for a snappy comeback or perhaps even a push to move him out of her orbit. Instead, she reached out a hand and grasped his shoulder all while she rose up on her toes and pressed her mouth to his.

Shocked at her actions, he failed to react for a few beats. Such tender lips, so sweet. The unexpected caress had him reeling, so when she drew back, still frowning, he took only a moment to decide return the gesture, and he wouldn't be nearly so chaste about it.

"See, I can be—"

He stopped her protest with a kiss of his own, circling one of his hands around the back of her head as he allowed the other to drop to her waist as he took over. With only a few nudging encouragements, she'd opened her mouth to him, allowing him to taste her, tease with his tongue in a new way as she quivered in his grasp. With a pent-up little moan she leaned against him, her breasts firmly pressed to his chest. His cock, which had been on alert since he'd first touched Teah, now sprang to near-painful attention.

Teah kissed him back, her little nips and licks the only encouragement he needed to lift her up and press her against the wall of the building sheltering them. He grabbed at her thighs and pulled them around his waist even as he ground his hips into her, his thickened cock sliding along the plump flesh between her legs. All the residual adrenaline from the fight ignited in his veins as he allowed sexual energy build between them. He wished he'd removed his damned gloves so he could finally grasp some of her curves.

She made a soft sound deep in her throat and clutched harder at his shoulders, her tongue teasing his then retreating to the safety of her mouth. He followed with a foray of his own and her whole body softened against his as he thrust his tongue inside her. A sudden flash of awareness filled him: Teah would melt against him when he penetrated her. She was incredibly responsive and he was certain when they finally had intercourse, it would be a fulfilling encounter. The way she suddenly clamped her thighs around him and rocked her pussy against the ridge of his cock only confirmed it.

The sudden chirrup of his alarm startled him, and he pulled away from Teah's succulent lips, the need to return to duty overriding arousal in a painful snap. Teah's head fell back and she blinked groggily as he answered his comm link summons. An emergency required as much of his attention he could provide even though he was in the middle of foreplay.

"Hey, Eidan! How'd the fight go?" His sister's voice rang out in a cheerful query, and he winced. No emergency, just inopportune curiosity.

"I won."

At his brief answer, Teah focused on him, then glanced down their tightly entwined bodies. A deeper blush rose up her cheeks, and she pressed at his forearms and wriggled her legs. Her movements were quite stimulating—everything about her was stimulating in fact, but it was clear she was trying to escape him yet again. In response, he tightened his grip on her full buttocks and she let out a tiny squeal.

"What was that? Are you still at the location? Do you need me to escort you out?"

"No." He included Teah in that denial. She was staying exactly where she was. The woman in his arms sucked in a breath and pushed at his chest. He flinched because she happened to compress a new bruise and he almost lost his grip on her. She took advantage of his divided attention and kicked her legs. His cock appreciated the rhythmic motion.

"Let me down," she whispered with a scowl.

"Who was that?" Brida asked quickly. No longer willing to put up with eavesdropping, Eidan reluctantly removed one of his hands from the lush curve of Teah's ass and hit private link on the comm. Now his sister wouldn't be able to hear anything but his voice. As soon as he let go of her, Teah struggled in earnest and with an agile twist she was free, ducking under his arm as he reached for her.

"Was there anything else?" he asked as he followed Teah along the walk. She picked up the pace, and he allowed himself the luxury of watching her hips sway.

"Not really. Just checking in to make sure my little brother hadn't gotten his skull cracked open by some smelly human savage."

At these words, Teah spun around suddenly, a thunderous frown on her face. "*Smelly* human *savage*?"

"You're not a savage," Eidan tried to reassure her, though the idea of Teah sinking her teeth into him as they engaged in a naked tussle definitely brought out the primal in him.

"Who's a savage?" Brida asked.

"No one's a savage." He nearly shouted it, frustrated that Teah wasn't touching him and that his sister had used such a derogatory term so openly. Yes, they had joked about how primitive human society seemed, but it wouldn't do to entertain even superficial judgments now that they were here among their new constituents. "Brida, I'm signing off."

With a jerk of his hands he shut off the link and faced his peeved human.

"Don't even think it." Teah warned him off with a raised hand. She shuffled backward and eyed him like he was armed and dangerous.

"You don't know what I'm thinking." Eidan knew it was a lie, the bulge in his trousers clearly advertising what he was after.

Teah shook her head. "Do all Eleoni disdain humans, or is it just you and your sister?"

"I don't dislike humans and neither does Brida—"

She huffed out an aggrieved breath. "Don't even think about following me!"

With that pronouncement she spun and continued her flight. Teah didn't hold back in telling him what to do. Eidan let her go, guessing that she was no longer in an amorous or conciliatory frame of mind.

****

Teah wanted to cry. Or kick something. At least that man wasn't following her like he tended to do, hounding her and monitoring her like she was feebleminded. Dismay and desire stewed in her gut, and she let out a grunt of frustration as she thudded up her stairs, intent on retreating to her little home. It was well past time to return, Broose needed to be fed, her cooking supplies needed reorganizing…

Once she had her door safely closed and her aircuttle soothed to a soft violet shade, she turned to her kitchen. Organizing her cleansers, she set to work wiping down cabinets and arranging her few pots and pans by size and purpose. Broose kept sneaking in wherever she was working and picking up things to drop with a clang whenever she noticed him. Teah tried to keep her mind away from Eidan, but it was as impossible a task as keeping the mud at bay in the postal station below her.

So the sheriff thought she was a savage. And smelly. The arrogance and bigotry confounded her. She'd done nothing to provoke such an opinion. Granted, a fair portion of the population of Rusk tended to be rancid, and there was a higher proportion of the uncouth among its inhabitants, but *she* hadn't behaved badly. With a start she remembered how she'd initiated that reckless kiss. Well, to be honest, it hadn't really left her mind at any point, just as Eidan's passionate response had lingered despite her best efforts to forget it. She'd finally discovered that his beard was soft and springy, not coarse as she'd feared. The idea that she'd been so willingly spread-eagled against a building by his body, where anyone could see, was so out of character she wondered at her sanity.

He'd kissed her back, so what did that say about *his* taste? If he thought she was some barbarian with bad breath, why had he—

A sudden wail from outside startled her, and she spun towards the sound. It was unfamiliar, but its constant mechanical tone indicated it was some sort of emergency beacon. She heard a few shouts from the street, and was on her feet and struggling into her boots before she quite knew what she was doing. Broose circled overhead, fluttering with agitation at the unexpected activity. She usually had much quieter evenings with him, but since Eidan and his snobby sister had landed, it seemed things were shaking up forward and aft.

After herding her aircuttle back into the apartment, she secured the door and stood on her landing to reconnoiter, the alarm much louder now. To the west she could see a bright orange glow with thick grey smoke lifting from it. A fire, in the entertainment section. She rattled down the steps and made her way through the darkening streets, getting caught up in a group of other residents making their way to the scene. Rounding a corner, she finally saw what was happening. The Last Chance Gambling Parlor was in flames. Hot red and gold flickers crept up the side of the building, curling almost to the low roof as thick gouts of blackish smoke rolled out from under the eaves. She could feel the heat on her skin even from this distance. Most people stood in a loose semi-circle around the conflagration, well back from the action, as a few people rushed close then leaped back, buckets dangling from their hands as they failed to extinguish it. At least Dorian wasn't working that evening.

Teah wracked her brain, unsure what sort of fire suppression organization even existed in Rusk. It rained so much she'd never really considered the possibility.

"Do we have some equipment?" she asked a group of nearby bystanders who either stared at her blankly or shrugged their shoulders, apparently too caught up in the spectacle to be bothered. Screwing up her courage, she approached the few who seemed to be fighting the fire and offered to help. One soot-smudged woman Teah recognized as a friend of Dorian's, indicated a mismatched jumble of buckets and a streaming hose winding down from a nearby rooftop cistern. She set to righting buckets and filling them and found willing hands snatching them up as soon as they were ready.

The fire grew bolder, and she could hear its roar as it began to consume the eave of the roof. It didn't seem like their puny efforts were making any impact. More people approached for water, and she looked up from her task to see Eidan and his sister standing there, waiting to take up the next two. Without acknowledging either, she kept going, keeping one wary eye on the progress of the flames. One after the other she filled buckets, mud splashing up her legs as volunteers dropped more at her side. Just as she wondered if she'd be able to go on or if the cistern was close to empty, cool humidity pressed away some of the ferocious heat filling the air. With a soft hiss, Rusk returned to its usual weather and rain began to fall, softly at first, then in a steady patter. Many of the spectators wandered away to take places under convenient overhangs and roof edges, but Teah kept working. Eidan and Brida did not let up on their efforts either. Both Eleoni were machine-like as they repetitively threw water at the flames.

As the rain increased to a downpour, the fire finally began to retreat, steam rising through the roof as the glow of the combustion lessened and finally died. The gambling den was half consumed. Blackened walls and yawing holes where windows and doors had once been were all that remained of the front corner of the building. She barely noticed the rain dampening her hair and trickling down the back of her neck. She straightened up from her half-crouch slowly. With the immediate danger past, she noticed how shaky she was. The adrenaline that had flooded her body was now leaving her light-headed and unsteady on her feet.

"Why are you here?" Eidan's stern voice broke through her fog, and she turned to find him looming behind her, shoving used buckets out of the way with his booted feet. Despite just seeing him at the fights, her heart shivered in her chest like she'd missed him for days. Irritation with his high-handedness bloomed anew.

"Because I wanted to help. Some of us dirty barbarians have altruistic impulses."

He hissed out an impatient breath and gave one harsh shake of his head. "She's going to apologize for that comment. After we conclude our inspection of the scene."

Dwelling on his insult subsided as she realized what he was saying. "You think this was deliberate?"

He clamped his mouth shut and retreated behind his beard and Eleoni hauteur. "You need to go home."

"*You* need to stop giving me orders." The aggressive reply was out of her mouth before she realized what she was saying.

"I wouldn't have to give orders if people behaved in a reasonable manner. *Go home.*"

Teah couldn't help her chin jutting out or her shoulders straightening as she prepared to face off with the man she'd been wrapped around only an hour before. The man who'd made her so hot she still ached. He was insufferable, and she wasn't going to put up with his rude manner, sheriff of an entire planet or not. Just as she drew in a deep breath to attack, his sister walked up and greeted him with a quick salute.

"Sheriff, I secured the perimeter and did a quick scan, but it's too dark to do a thorough visual inspection."

"Morning is soon enough for that. We can review the data back at the station." Eidan hadn't taken his eyes off Teah as he replied to Brida, and the other woman noticed his glare with raised eyebrows.

"Hello, Teah. I didn't have a chance before to say thanks for helping out earlier," the officer said in a friendly tone. Teah gave her a cold look.

"I'll just be going," she spat out and turned away.

"That's excellent," Eidan shot back.

"I'm not going because you told me to."

"The result is the same." His reply was fainter as she kept walking. At least that meant he wasn't following her, as usual.

"What's going on?" Brida's confused question was the last Teah heard as she rushed off into the night, grateful to leave the Eleoni far behind.

Chapter Four

"But I already have the standard fire suppression and detection equipment installed in here." Teah's impatient tone matched the frown she was wearing. Eidan ignored her, at least as well as he was able. He was too busy balancing on a ladder as he affixed an upgraded monitoring routine to the post office security system to reply anyway. Besides, if he spoke to her, he'd look at her, then he'd want to strip her clothes off and tell her to kiss him and that sort of scene shouldn't be enacted in the middle of the post office lobby.

"This module is the latest version and improves photoelectric detection by fourteen percent. I'm also going to tweak your isotopes a bit more. These aren't functioning at peak efficiency."

"You're going to tweak my isotopes?"

He looked away from the small device mounted to the ceiling of the building and spared her a glance. Teah was wearing her uniform, regrettably, and her brows were raised as she stared up at him. Speculating on the details of her nude body was distracting, but it was all his brain seemed to be able to do other than worry over the details of the previous evening's fire. It had been arson, as he'd suspected. Chemical accelerant trails were clearly visible on the remaining structures. Probably retaliation for failure to pay protection money or a rival gambling hall's attempt to cut out competition. Since Eidan didn't have much of a system of informants set up yet, he was doing his investigation the old fashioned way by having his human officers interview people, and inventory supplies of the fuel that had been used. He should probably be out amongst the population, but he had a feeling the ill will most humans harbored for Eleoni would have a quieting effect on any potential witness. So he was here, at the post office, improving this bastion of Collective government's security as Brida attended to making similar upgrades to the medical building just down the street.

"Yes, I'm going to tweak your isotopes and manipulate your photoelectric cell."

She flung out her hands and paced around the base of the ladder. "I didn't ask you to do this. It isn't necessary. No one's going to set a torch to this place. It holds all sorts of things people have paid a great deal of money to have shipped here. Whoever tried would be run out of town."

Eidan stopped staring at her honey colored hair, which he wanted to uncoil from the braid she had pinned to the top of her head. He'd like to pull those silky strands across his skin, feel them slither along his belly as she took his hard cock into that warm mouth of hers. Shaking his head, he narrowed his eyes at the blinking red and green lights of the monitor.

"As sheriff, it falls within my purview to make such security adjustments I judge necessary for the protection of Collective property or personnel."

"And as postal officer of record, I must approve any modifications that are made to this structure. I can look up the statute if you require an exact citation."

Eidan smiled at her ready comeback. She must have been brushing up on legal codes since he'd arrived. "No need, I know the regulation. And you are very well aware my authority supersedes yours in this case."

"And you love that," she muttered under her breath, and he concentrated very hard on flipping the correct switches rather than laughing at her outrage. He knew it wouldn't do to tease her when she was still fuming from Brida's quip. His sister really needed to deliver that apology so he could get back to the business of wooing this woman into his bed in his off hours. It was going to be a challenge, but one with a sure-to-be delicious reward. It had been a while since he'd conducted an affair, and he looked forward to the excitement and pleasure. Eleoni women were usually quite straightforward in their interest, and both parties would end the association on good terms when no meld was achieved. He'd never strayed from his own kind, so had no idea what he'd have to do to first seduce a human, and keep her interested afterward.

A quick check of his handheld device compared to the readings of the building system reassured him that his work was done on this level. "Now we need to go upstairs and take care of your living quarters—"

"Absolutely not!" She stuck out her chin and gave one firm shake of her head.

"Why not?"

"Your official capacities do not extend to invading my private space, Sheriff."

Eidan stepped down from the ladder and watched as she retreated behind her counter. "Should I write up a search warrant in order to gain entry? That's within my purview as well."

She flushed and looked down, grabbing up a cloth and wiping at her spotless counter in rapid strokes. "You wouldn't dare."

"I would on the flimsiest of pretexts." He leaned across the counter and got as close to her as the barrier permitted, liking how she didn't retreat any further but instead retrieved a bottle of cleanser and sprayed it close to his arm. She attacked the wet surface with rough circles of the wadded cloth. He wanted to pull her over and nibble the tunic right off of her as she squealed, but again, this wasn't the place. "But I think I'll wait to be invited."

At the little sally she looked up from her pointless task and gave him a glare. "In that case, you'll be waiting for the Madrigal star field to freeze over."

He laughed. That particular star cluster spanned the width of a galaxy and was unlikely to suffer any white stars or black holes so early in its development. Give it a few billion years.

"Don't laugh at me. You're being patronizing."

"No, I'm not. Weren't you trying to make me laugh?"

"I meant it. The last thing I'd want is you in there, agitating, agitating … my aircuttle."

He caught up the cloth and tugged at it. She scowled and pulled back. "Give me that."

"You don't need it. This counter is clean enough for surgery."

"Just trying to keep the smell of us savages from your privileged nose." Her brown eyes flared bright.

"I never said you were a savage." He continued to pull on her cloth, and Teah, stubborn creature that she was, refused to relent, and ended up leaning his way as he flexed his arm. Her face was close to his and he watched her features flicker from an annoyed frown to confusion, then to something softer as her tightened lips eased. How could he resist another kiss?

****

Teah quivered from her scalp to her toenails. Eidan Cozad was driving her insane. First his barging in and taking over security for her building, then his taunting and teasing on top of it. Now he was practically dragging her over the counter by playing this silly game with her dusting cloth. The humorous light faded from his lavender eyes and a sudden pulse of heat burst through her body like a comet's trail. She'd seen that look, just before he'd—

Eidan's mouth settled against hers as quickly as his hands reached out and caught her shoulders. Nips at her upper and lower lips had them tingling and swollen, and within a heated second his tongue was sliding into her mouth, teasing and sure even as his grip on her tightened. Everything melted inside, and she wanted to crawl across the counter to get closer to him. Her pussy clenched with enough force to make her gasp against his mouth and he drew back, a knowing smile on those wicked lips.

"You're going to invite me in. In fact, you're going to be begging me."

Teah wanted to put up an aggrieved rebuttal. "I've never begged for anything."

He stopped her feeble assertion with another kiss, this one slower and deeper, made more arousing by the way he slid his fingers into her hair and tugged ever so gently. A rattle startled her, and Eidan released her so suddenly she swayed. He took a step back from the counter, his eyes looking her over as she gaped at him, then glanced over his shoulder to see a large Kotze miner bending over to take off her boots.

"I'll just be checking the transponder on your delivery cart out back. Have to make sure Collective property is properly tagged and secure."

Teah couldn't speak, could only watch him swagger out the front door after giving the miner a brief nod of greeting. A strand of hair fell from her upsweep, and she tucked it back as best she could as she tried to compose herself to get back to work.

Chapter Five

It was early evening, and Eidan was trying to appreciate his constituents as he strolled down the main thoroughfare with Brida, but it was difficult. They attracted stares, most neutral, but far too many hostile for his comfort. He hadn't anticipated being welcomed with open arms, but he'd hoped his fighting demonstration would have garnered him a bit more respect among the brawling population. Then again, his day had been spent putting the contents of three illegal pharmaceutical manufacturing sites to the torch, so his popularity would be taking a beating among the drug-addled and their dealers. At least it wasn't raining.

He and his sister were going out to dinner before trading shifts at the security station, and they'd decided to eat at a local restaurant rather than at home where they could prepare Eleoni dishes they favored. Part of coming to understand humans and Kotze had to include becoming familiar with their cuisine. They were going to a place called the Henderson, upon the recommendation of a thin deputy named Jawson.

They reached the doors of the establishment, a small illuminated sign advertising what was within, as well as the scents of food wafting through the door as people entered and left. Eidan followed Brida in, her instinct to survey the space before him compelling her to step ahead. They found a long, low ceilinged room filled with mismatched chairs and tables, a narrow bar area along one wall and the back of the space holding a few gaming stations. The humans and Kotze in attendance looked up at the Eleoni, but then went back to their conversations and meals with little remark.

Brida located an empty table in a corner that would provide cover for their backs and took a seat after removing her coat. Eidan joined her and took a look over the menu display mounted to the center of the table with a few rusty bolts. The human dishes looked very bland and basic, and he strained to find something that might satisfy him. He spared a few seconds speculation on what sorts of foods Teah liked, then realized having a meal with her would be the perfect way to discover her palate and more aspects to her personality. Now he had to discover a way to convince her to spend time with him.

They input their selections with Brida muttering under her breath about how everything was either fried or made from flour. Back to a sour mood, it seemed.

"How are you feeling? Having a bad moment?" Eidan was anxious for his sister to recover from her broken meld. She needed to have her hormones return to single levels, for living without the company of one's melded partner could drive an Eleoni to depression or desperate acts. Just before they'd left Eleon, Brida's man had declared he wasn't going to follow or wait for her and had gone to the physician to start separation treatment. His sister, stubborn to the end, had declared she'd allow the chemical alterations her love had made upon her to leach from her cells naturally, but the process was taking some time.

Watching her suffer had reinforced Eidan's determination to avoid melding. It was a primitive and uncontrolled process he didn't want to undergo no matter how lovely the woman might be. Being stationed so far from potential partners was a blessing. He doubted a human would provoke his body in such a way. He'd never heard of an Eleoni-human meld before. All the more reason to pursue Teah. They could simply enjoy each other freely with no lasting repercussions.

"I don't know. Some days I feel like myself, and then suddenly a smell or sound sets me off, reminds me of everything I've lost and I get shaky and hot. It's miserable." Brida sighed, and inspected the knife included with the flatware bundle on the table. "Although I've reached the point where if I saw Wil, I'd be inclined to stab him rather than kiss him."

"I suppose that's an improvement."

Eidan glanced around the room and noticed several people gathering up their belongings and leaving, even though they didn't seem to have finished their meals. Fewer diners made it easy to pick out the three large men suddenly approaching their table. There was no mistaking their intent focus on him and his sister. Eidan's adrenaline ratcheted up as he assessed the threat standing in front of him, trusting Brida to evaluate their surroundings and scan for an ambush from the sides. At least their backs were protected by a wall of synthetic steel.

For a brief instant, he wondered if there would be some verbal threats or posturing first, but that notion disappeared when the man in the center picked up a suddenly vacated chair. It was clear at the outset he and Brida were facing mere brawlers, slabby men more used to using muscle and weight rather than skill or precision to settle matters.

Eidan leapt to his feet as Brida pushed the table towards their attackers. Then he blocked the first swing with his elbow and quickly backed away to alter the balance of the second man and pull him over onto his face. As that man skidded across the dirty floor with a curse, Eidan headed off a flurry of blows aimed haphazardly at him by the first fellow. He had no idea what Brida was doing, but judging by the sound of fists striking flesh and human male howls of pain, she was succeeding at whatever esoteric bit of hand-to-hand technique she was practicing on the hapless outlaw.

As the downed man squirmed on the floor and tried to grab at Eidan's leg, the other aimed a kick at his midsection in a poorly planned coordinated assault. Eidan broke the fallen man's knee with one well-placed stomp and turned fast enough to miss most of the force of the other's kick. Before he could gather himself for an attack, Brida flew past him in a blur and struck his attacker with a rolling kick to the jaw that sent the other man's head back in a black-out snap. He toppled down next to his screaming friend, and Eidan looked around for anyone else caring to take a turn. The crowd that had gathered to watch the drama stayed far out of reach, all avidly taking in the scene. One young woman calmly poured herself a mug of beer from a pitcher at her table and gave him a wink.

Knowing he needed to present himself and Collective behavior as well as possible at this juncture, Eidan did not break any necks as he looked over the writhing criminals littering the ground. Brida's first victim was sprawled against a pile of overturned chairs, his broken arm hanging at a bizarre angle as some sort of spilled stew dripped down his shirt front. The other two men also clearly needed medical attention. Eidan cuffed the man with the destroyed knee as well as the one who was still unconscious while Brida used her comm link to call the medical clinic and request some assistance.

Eidan knelt next to the man with the broken arm and searched him for weapons, ignoring his epithet-laden protests. He discovered a projectile weapon and two blades.

"Why didn't you use this?" Eidan asked, as he dropped the devices into an evidence bag he kept in a pocket for just these sorts of occasions.

"Too easy," the attacker wheezed as he tried to lift his arm into a more secure position.

Eidan refrained from commenting, that from his perspective, foiling this amateurish ambush had certainly been very easy.

"Who paid you?"

His opponent rolled his eyes, and Eidan couldn't help but grin. The rush from combat was still flowing through him, and he almost wished another opponent intent on mayhem would burst out of the crowd. Brida would likely get to him first, though. He couldn't find any identity chips on any of the men, so discovering who they were would have to wait until their medical scans.

His sister approached his side and looked over her handiwork.

"It seems as if someone is taking the direct approach this time," he said and Brida nodded.

"Does this mean we can skip our meal here?"

****

Teah knew she should have said no. She should have come up with some excuse such as needing to sort packages or dust the ceiling or reorganize her closet, but in the end she'd been so flabbergasted by Eidan Cozad's invitation to dinner she'd simply said yes. He'd come to the post office and stood at the counter when he'd asked right in front of two Kotze who were collecting their shipments of custom entertainment chips from their home planet. Perhaps she'd been too flustered to think in a more agile way under the steady regard of the two aliens who watched her and Eidan's interchange with deep interest. So she'd said yes, he'd smiled, and had immediately turned on his heel and exited the post office, on to his next bit of community relations.

He'd sent further instruction via a personal message, and she'd arrived at his and his sister's house that evening not sure what to expect. She'd been surprised to find Brida was out, working the night shift, and had contemplated making an excuse and leaving while she could. But somehow she hadn't spoken the words, and was now standing in the Eleoni kitchen, feeling awkward as Eidan nimbly chopped something leafy and green into tiny shreds.

"Thank you for inviting me." She glanced around the kitchen to find nearly every surface covered with platters of ingredients, bowls and implements laid out precisely, and all the heating elements on the stove supporting pots of simmering somethings. Tantalizing scents filled the air, and she inhaled, trying to identify some of the aromas. Growing up in a group home had been safe and well-managed, but there hadn't been funds for anything other the basic government food allotments. She couldn't identify much of anything.

"You're welcome. It seemed like the best thing to do to apologize for my comments." Eidan's gaze met hers for a moment, and something sparkled in their depths. Was he making fun of her again?

"Brida already said she was sorry about the smelly savage quip. And I get it. She meant people get mean and sweaty when they're in combat." Eidan hadn't been mean after that fight. He'd been very amorous, and remembering his musky scent made her breath come up short. Since she hadn't been involved in any altercation, she wasn't sure what *her* excuse was.

The overhead lights made Eidan's long auburn hair glow like burnished copper. He had the strands wound into a loose bun on the back of his head, and as he worked over something red on the cutting board, she wondered how long it was. Longer than hers?

"Considering my last attempt to eat out in public, I decided it would be more peaceful to dine in this evening."

Teah nodded. News of the fight had spread through the community rapidly. She'd woken up that morning with a message from Dorian that had included a brief snippet of video taken at Henderson's that showed the last few seconds. Eidan and his sister had battled back their attackers with grim efficiency. Rumors were rampant about who was to blame for incident. "Did you discover why they were mad at you?"

Eidan laughed and tossed some tiny whitish cubes into a hot pan. They sizzled and released a pungent scent into the air as he stirred with a long metal spoon. Teah was still trying to absorb the fact that the man she'd watched pummel others was making her dinner, and a very elaborate dinner at that.

"Assassination attempts are usually not motivated by emotion, other than rage. I feel it was a pragmatic action on their part, however."

Her stomach lurched, then tightened. "You mean they meant to kill you, right from the start?"

"Of course," he replied as he added a handful of bright orange shreds to the mixture in the hot pan, then poured in some sort of broth.

She gripped the edge of the counter as a wave of shock poured over her. Murdering Eidan and Brida, two official lawgivers from the Collective? Who in Rusk would have the short-sighted temerity to undertake such a thing? The ramifications would be swift and punitive for all the humans here. Another thought soon followed. Was the Marshal's untimely death a homicide?

"Who? *Why*?" Thinking about the man in front of her, so vitally alive, bleeding out on the muck-smeared floor of a dive like Henderson's made her blood run cold.

"That's the question I intend to answer," he said before peering at her with a frown. "What's this? You're pale. You need to sit."

Teah opened her mouth to protest, but failed to produce a sound, still dwelling on the concept of a deceased Eidan Cozad. She'd foolishly assumed the confrontation had been prompted by some cultural misunderstanding like she and Eidan found themselves embroiled in every time they spoke. But deliberate murder was a whole other story.

He maneuvered her closer to him as he studied her face. Then before she realized what he was doing, she was hoisted up onto a clear space on the counter. His hands lingered on her hips as he spoke.

"Stay there, where I can observe you."

Summoning up some bravado, hoping to repress her sudden worry for him, she pushed back. "Afraid I'm going to do something illegal right under your nose?"

"Petrified." Despite his near-death experience, he was still as arrogant as ever. He quirked a smile at her and pressed his fingertips into the soft flesh of her hips. "Consider this evening as my attempt to contain you and keep the streets of Rusk safe for all the innocents wandering about."

She laughed. She couldn't help it. "So you're going to be watching my every move? Ready to pounce on any infraction?"

He made a low sound in his throat and leaned even closer, his nose mere centimeters from hers. A drift of his scent eased into her nostrils, and her toes curled. He ran his palms down her thighs, and she resisted the aching urge to spread her legs and wrap them around him. "Exactly. So be on your best behavior tonight."

He turned away to stir something bubbling on the stove, and Teah took in a shaky breath as she tried to cool off her roaring hormones. She'd already kissed him. It didn't mean she was going to follow up with anything more intense.

"Why are you here?"

"You invited me."

He shot her an assessing look at her quick response, then returned to stripping small, pungent leaves from a twig. "I meant here in Rusk."

Teah told herself to relax and make conversation with him. He was being polite at the moment, and she wanted to encourage that behavior. It was so much more pleasant than bickering. "I decided I wanted to join the civil service as soon as I learned about it. I was eight, and there was a big announcement about us encountering the Eleoni on Vega. As a child, it seemed like a great adventure to go into space. Plus it gave me hope for a better future, away from the group home. Something to work towards."

"And as an adult? Have you found Civil Service a … great adventure?"

"It's a wonderful opportunity." She went silent as she considered the alternative. If she'd stayed on Earth, remained in her neighborhood, she'd be working in a windowless factory for starvation wages while facing a short life span, or worse.

Eidan gathered up the chopped herb and placed it in a tiny bowl just the right size. He handed it over, and she took a sniff of the peppery fragrance. "Please enlighten me as to the wonders of Rusk. I seem to have missed them under all the mud."

She laughed. "I admit it's not much to look at. The weather is foul, and many of the people aren't especially friendly—"

"Attributes which enhance its appeal in an incredible way," he shot back with a slight smile. Teah handed him the bowl, and he slid it to the side of the cutting board.

"But it's the frontier, a brand new place. Not Earth." All her excitement about being part of humanity's foray into trans-galactic space, of having a secure, respectable job, faded slightly as she considered how bleak her life had been. Without a pale future before her, she never would have had the determination and courage to study constantly, take the placement tests, and get though the interview process to join the Collective civil service. The Eleoni had decided to open up a few positions for humans in their bureaucracy as a way to integrate this new species into their system, and she still thrilled with pride whenever she realized she'd made it.

"Not Earth?"

Teah shook her head and absently accepted a sprig of another herb he handed over. She rubbed the velvety leaf between her fingers, and it released a strong citrus odor. "There wasn't much of a future for me there. In order to succeed, have some security, what matters are family connections and how much money you have. I didn't have either, so the opportunity to achieve something for myself was something I couldn't pass up."

"No family?"

She shook her head, remembering the sterile, shabby group home, the barely-acknowledged holidays, worn clothes, minimal meals. At least the managers had kept them safe and they'd been able to go to school. That was more than many children could count on. Such melancholy thoughts had no place here in this warm and fragrant kitchen as she watched an extremely attractive man chop up a bumpy yellow vegetable.

"What about you? Why are you here?" Enough about her. She'd left all that behind.

"Orders." The clipped way he said it indicated this was not a good subject, so she left it by the wayside.

"What are you making?"

"Some Eleon dishes. Basic things for you to try." He rattled off a few names that meant nothing to her, and she watched him work. He cooked with the same confident efficiency that he'd demonstrated in his fight, and the sight of his strong, lean hands mixing colorful vegetables and wielding a flashing knife was strangely absorbing.

"I'll try anything." Teah winced inwardly. That sounded provocative. At least Eidan didn't react to it. "I have a pretty limited range of cooking skills which fits the minimal choices of food at the market."

With that, he picked up a small spoon and dipped it into the velvety sauce he'd been whipping. He held it in front of her lips and she tried to take the handle, but he narrowed his eyes and shook his head. "Our dishes are based on a balance of flavors and texture. Something creamy with something crunchy, something salty with something sweet. *Orant* with umami. Open."

His lavender eyes were flashing a challenge, and a moment before she relented, Teah understood this evening was going to change things irrevocably between them. A soft, aroused part of herself reveled in this knowledge as her more rational side declared she'd fight it. Resist him. She opened her mouth. He eased the spoon in, not taking his eyes from her as he watched her react.

The sauce was rich and flavorful, a faint hint of some spice underpinning the creaminess. With something like that as a topper, she could see herself eating an old boot with relish. Licking off the bowl of the spoon, she released it from her mouth, and Eidan watched the whole process intently.

"You liked it?"

"I did," she whispered wishing she could look away from him, desperate for her body to cool, for her lungs to expand to their correct volume.

"That was *ilkit*, a basic accompaniment to vegetables. How about you try … this."

Now he swooped a different spoon her way, this one laden with a tiny heap of bright green spheres. Again he commanded her to open, and again she obeyed before she could tell herself not to. Smoky, tangy pricks of flavor pebbled across her tongue as the tiny balls disintegrated on contact with her mouth, and she involuntarily gasped at the strange sensation.

He smiled at her reaction. "And that was *terap*, the roe of a sea serpent. A basic condiment on Eleon. We put it on everything."

Snake eggs? "How did you get them?"

"We have them delivered. There happens to be a very reliable postal service on this planet." His compliment was delivered in a low tone and accompanied by an intent look.

"No, I meant how do you get them from the snake?" She tried to laugh, to deflect some of this tension building deep inside her body, coiling in all the places she ignored and kept secret from herself.

"I've never considered the question before. I would imagine the female requires some gentle persuading." He swept his fingertips along her jaw, and her pussy clenched. She longed to thrust her fingers into his carefully restrained hair, longed to have him push between her legs as he fastened his mouth to her neck. He was an alien, a practical stranger, a dangerous man, and he made her desperate.

He stepped away suddenly, and she went cold, despite the warmth from the stove flooding the kitchen. After rummaging in a cabinet, Eidan emerged with a small black glass bottle and two tiny crystal flutes. He poured out two measures of a shimmery grey liquid and offered her one. She sipped it without prompting and immediately winced in pain as the substance burned along her taste buds. Putting the glass down as quickly as she could, she waved a hand in front of her mouth as she coughed. The liquid had a distinctive piney flavor that lingered long after she'd swallowed.

Eidan handed her a glass of water, and she quickly drank it down. It diluted the flavor of the liquor, and it was suddenly quite pleasant, filling her mouth with an herbal tang.

"I'm sorry, I meant to warn you to wait until you had water. You are supposed to drink them together as an aperitif." Eidan was in front of her, his hand reaching out to cup her cheek. His skin was warm against hers, and she stared at him as he stroked a thumb at the corner of her mouth.

"Did it burn your tongue? It's a very caustic flavor for the uninitiated."

"I think I'm all right."

"It's supposed to stimulate the appetite, but perhaps I've damaged yours." He peered at her, and her skin burned wherever he touched it. He brushed his fingertips across her lips, and she fought the impulse to suck one right into her mouth.

"I'm still hungry."

"But are you famished, Teah Riuda?" Eidan's voice dropped into that low purr she was coming to recognize and delight in.

Something hot glowed in the air between them, and she tried to gauge his intentions. Was he teasing her like before, or was he serious as he'd been during their brief encounter after the fight? She'd flung herself at him then, to arousing if confusing results, and if she did it now and he laughed, she'd be too humiliated to ever look him in the eye again.

Her throat was too dry to speak so she managed to nod her head once. He leaned her way, his hard abdomen pressing against her knees. The lightheaded feeling she was experiencing had nothing to do with physical hunger.

He pressed his hands to the counter on either side of her hips and looked at her mouth.

"Isn't this the moment where you usually kiss me?"

Oh, the boldness of this man amazed her. "I hardly consider doing something once constitutes a *habit*."

"So it's going to be only once? And I thought you enjoyed yourself."

"We humans can be difficult to predict."

"Makes dealing with you interesting." He made a soft sound deep in this throat, and her knees trembled. It was the evening of a long and busy day, they were alone, and this prickling heat that rose between them was a torment. Without worrying much more about it—after all, she had done it before to no ill effects—Teah leaned his way and brought her mouth close to his. Close enough to feel the heat of his skin against hers, to take in his rich scent.

"Not quite there, *alati*," he whispered, just before she stopped his words with her lips. Awareness and excitement pulsed through her as his warm mouth molded to hers and she wondered what had taken her so long. The hairs of his beard tickled her chin. His hands clutched at her thighs as he dragged her to the edge of the counter. With quick movements he had her knees parted, and it didn't take much time for her to welcome his weight between her legs, all while countering his sucks at her lips with more of her own. The herbal flavor of the drink mingled on their tongues.

As he pressed his pelvis to her sex, all her nerve endings went up in flames and she gasped out with surprise. He was hard, so hard she could feel the dimensions of his cock through his clothes and hers.

Without volition, her toes curled and her knees slid higher along his sides, her body automatically welcoming him in as close as possible. With a little grumble he pulled away from her mouth and stared at her for a moment, his lavender eyes darkened to deep purple. As he pulled his hands from her body and stepped back, her mouth fell open with shock. Was that it? Maybe there was some sort of Eleoni foreplay ritual she'd misunderstood.

With a few quick punches of his fingers, Eidan turned off all the heating elements under his various pots and pans and slid his knives into the sink. He then stepped back to her and scooped her up in his arms, holding her tight to his hard chest as he walked from the kitchen area.

"What … where are we going?" She supposed she should have put up some protest and struggled to regain her footing, but his tight hold on her felt too reassuring to lose.

"Away from hard surfaces, high temperatures, and sharp edges."

All very safety minded concerns. He was the sheriff after all, and her well-being would be a priority. They approached the huge, soft sofa and she prepared to be lowered down, but he kept walking, heading into a dim corridor in the opposite side of the house. She clutched at his shoulders, awareness of his likely destination flooding her with nerves and arousal at the same time.

She didn't have time to formulate a logical question before he'd carried her in to a dark room and stood her up on her shaky legs. He found her mouth unerringly and kissed her deeply, all while his hands roamed over her body, cupping her breasts, bumping her tight nipples, sliding down her sides to clutch at her buttocks. A throb built in her groin, pulsing out to her pussy and up to her chest in staccato bursts.

"Take off my clothes," he whispered.

"You don't give me orders," Her rebuttal was weak, weakened even further by her traitorous hands quick flutter to the fastenings of his shirt. The snaps parted easily, with little cracking sounds that made her jump.

"You like it." He stopped talking and instead focused his mouth on her neck, running his teeth and lips along her pulse, then latching on with a gentle suck that made her breath flutter out in a moan. Somehow his shirt was off and she could finally feel his skin. She ran her hands across his chest and encountered soft hair curling over thick muscles. Then her fingertips encountered tiny bumps in even lines. Scars? He twitched against her touch and another overwhelming bolt of heat flooded her.

"Take off my pants." Another order.

"Stop telling me what to do." Despite her defiance, she fumbled at the fastening to his trousers, momentarily confounded by the alien construction that seemed to involve cloth ties and some sort of self-sealing strip. He stopped licking her neck and reached down to help her, the garment falling to the floor after he eased it past his cock. In the fading light coming from the hallway, she could see it jutting out from his body, free of any sort of undergarment. One of his hands tickled down her arm to circle her wrist.

"Touch me."

"Why do you think you have to instruct me?"

"I know what I want."

"So do I." With those brave words, she reached out and curled her fingers around his erection, the silky skin covering his thick and pulsing flesh no different from the human men she'd encountered, even if his seemed harder and hotter. He shuddered out a groan, and she reveled in it, delighted to please him. She squeezed with her fingers as she rubbed along the tip, the smooth skin there making her fantasize about it sliding along the slippery folds of her pussy, teasing along every agonized and sensitive millimeter before finally thrusting inside.

"Then tell me." His command brought her up short, and she searched in the dim light to catch his expression.

"You'll follow *my* orders?"

"I'll comply with your requests. Within reason."

This all seemed like too much talking when she had a sexy man's cock warming her palm, so she went back to stoking him, allowing his arousal to ramp up her own. She hadn't taken a lover in her time on Rusk, and all the familiar sensations rushed back with a vengeance. It had been quite a while since she'd been so attracted to someone, and her spontaneity surprised her.

His hands went to her breasts, and the squeeze he gave them made her knees weak. With a little sigh of regret she released him and moved to unbutton her own tunic, but he stopped her.

"Let me learn."

She held still as he worked at her clothing, his request clearing her lust-hazed mind for a moment. "Have you been with a human woman before?"

He shook his head and tugged at her sleeves. "You're the first I've ever seen."

"I've never been with an Eleoni either." Her confession somehow eased her nerves and she stroked his shoulders, encountering more little bumps as he peeled away her pants, then rolled her underwear down.

"Then this will be a unique experience to share. A good test of human-Eleoni diplomacy." He nuzzled between her breasts, and she stumbled back, hitting the edge of what seemed to be his bed and tumbling backward onto a soft mattress topped with fluffy coverings. In an instant he was on top of her, pressing her down with his body as he took one of her distended nipples into his hot mouth. The instant relief of it made her shake and cry out.

Her legs parted, and he settled between them, one hand skating up the inside of her thigh. This was happening so fast she wasn't sure how much time had even elapsed, but slowing down would be like trying to hold back the tide. Her body thrummed with need, and she abandoned the last of her reservations as soon as his fingers touched her pussy. The exquisite sensation, something it seemed she'd been craving since she'd first seen Eidan, made her cry out. He stilled.

"Should I stop?"

"No!" She wriggled her hips, willing to do the work if he wasn't going to act. His cock bumped along her hip with every movement, and she fumbled to touch it, hampered by his strong arms framing her body.

He stroked her, fingertips running along her wet folds, finding all sorts of sensitive spots as she bucked and groaned. He rolled to his side and pulled her along with him, her leg thrown up over his hip, opening her to anything he cared to do. He nuzzled her shoulder while he stroked along one side of her swollen clit, then the other. His skills with her anatomy seemed to indicate Eleon women were constructed in a similar manner as humans. This was the last coherent thought she could entertain as he clenched his teeth in a gentle grasp on the point where her neck joined her shoulder all while running his fingers alongside her clit in an inexorable rhythm. His other arm snaked around her waist, and he clamped his hand on her ass tightly.

Her heart thudded as her body spun out of control while Eidan held her in place, helpless to move in his grip. She couldn't draw a deep breath, couldn't stop the harsh cries erupting from her throat. Sharp contractions bolted through her as climax slammed her muscles, everything tightening with incredible pleasure. She dug her fingers in his muscles, clawing at his back as she arched into him.

****

His cock throbbed. Eidan sucked in some deep breaths through his nose to calm himself, but that only brought the exquisite scent of Teah's arousal deeper into his brain. She shuddered in his arms, her breasts pressing into his chest, her soft and wet pussy quivering against his fingers as he teased her to a release. Again and again she jerked against his hand, her fingers digging into his back and shoulder.

Her sharp cries eased to soft moans as her movements quieted. He stopped stroking her clitoris, betting that just as for Eleon women, a human woman would be very sensitive after an orgasm. She shivered and stretched against him, her whole body melting into a soft, fragrant oasis. He wished there was a light on, for he wanted to see her naked, but rather than take his hands from her and activate any sort of illumination, he instead followed instinct as he'd been doing all along, and rolled her to her back, hoping she'd encourage him to penetrate her as he was desperate to do. She reached for his shoulders with a little murmur and slid her glorious thighs open, wrapping her legs around his waist without a moment's hesitation.

He reached for her pussy, grateful his earlier explorations had left him familiar with her, and circled his fingertip around the soft dent of her opening. She made a sharp sound and rocked her hips, which he interpreted as an invitation. He hitched his hips closer, his cock as hard as he'd ever experienced, and guided the head to her. At the first touch of her hot wet flesh he nearly spilled, groaning for control over his responses as he slowly pressed into her tight slippery sheath. Teah huffed out a breath and gave a low cry as she shifted her hips, grinding herself down on his cock before he could even thrust. One of her hands clenched at his ass as the other dug into his hair. He went still as something inside his brain clicked loose. He was suddenly so confused, so unsure, a feeling as foreign to him as running from a fight would be.

"Move, Eidan, please." Her throaty plead galvanized him, her splendid body warm and damp against his. His human needed him. Sucking in a steadying breath to counteract his sudden dizziness, he rolled his hips once, then again. Teah arched against him, rocking her pussy against his buried cock in counterpoint to his every thrust. Instinct ruled as he thrust hard against her, the tight, wet grip of her sheath stimulating him to increase his pace and build the sensation.

He told himself to slow down, touch her, shift position to give Teah more stimulation, but all he could do was bury himself deep in her sweetness, his skin already tingling the warning of his upcoming release. Before he could control himself, solid jolts of electric pleasure rocked through his straining body as his cum erupted from his cock. Shudders of pleasure worked through him as he emptied himself. As the pleasure receded into warm lethargy, waves of dizziness overcame him, and Eidan descended into the oblivion of sleep.

****

At least he wasn't snoring. Teah shifted in Eidan's bed, a blanket uncomfortably bunched under her back and his heavy arm weighting down her belly, preventing her from taking a deep breath. The air in his bedroom was cool, and her skin prickled. She longed to burrow under the coverings, curl up next to a nice warm body, but since he'd simply collapsed next to her after their frantic coupling without a kind word or even a caress, she didn't feel welcome to seek security in his arms.

She needed some comfort however. Uncertainty assailed her. She'd just done several impulsive things and was becoming more and more worried about the ramifications. It was certainly in character for her to act on a whim, but that usually meant wearing lacy foundations under her uniform or ordering something new in a restaurant, not having sexual intercourse with a man she barely knew. And not actually a man, either, but an Eleoni. She risked a glance at Eidan's bare form, barely visible in some reflected light from the hall, and that half a percent of DNA that separated human and Eleoni suddenly seemed too large. He was heavily muscled, perhaps the most physically imposing man she'd ever seen up close. There also seemed to be symmetrical stippling along the lines of his arms and abdomen, but it was difficult to distinguish in the shadowy room. Again, she wondered if they were some sort of ritualistic scarification. She was sure his normally stoic face was relaxed since he was sleeping deeply, his thick chest rising and falling with deep and steady exhalations. *He* wasn't fretting about what they'd done.

What sort of rules governed fraternization among Collective civil servants? She wasn't sure, and hadn't done any research mostly because she hadn't wanted to discover he was forbidden to her. Eidan was certainly well aware, but she wasn't going to wake him up and ask. Whatever the rules, she'd just made herself vulnerable, both to the whims of the sheriff and to the gossip and judgments of her fellow humans. Worry gnawed away the last of her pleasure from the orgasms he'd given her so unexpectedly, and she couldn't hold back her sigh. It didn't wake Eidan.

She rolled her head on the bed to tear her gaze from his shadowy profile and tried to see what was in his bedroom, but from her prone position, all she could make out was grey walls and two protruding lenses of what had to be bedside lamps. Those, and the bed beneath her naked body were all she could find. Did Eleoni prefer such sparse surroundings to fall asleep? The little she actually knew about Eidan and his race finally struck her, and she squeezed her eyes tightly shut as if to block out where she was and what she'd done.

She'd had sex with an alien. Really great sex, and with an incredibly impressive alien, but by no stretch of the imagination could she pretend he was anything other than irrevocably different from her and everything she knew. Her stomach roiled, and his arm lying over her, which previously been merely heavy, now seemed to press her down, confining her in a nearly frightening way. She let—no, she'd *begged*—for it, for him, had been desperate for him to touch her and invade her very essence. What had she been thinking?

Eidan kept sleeping, completely unaware of her presence. He didn't even roll on his side and tuck her closer to his body.

With sudden clarity, she knew what she had to do.

She wriggled her hips and dug her elbows into the soft bed, angling herself out from under his oppressive arm and sliding off the edge of the bed. She went still and peeked at Eidan. He shifted and rolled onto his side with a huffed breath. She looked at the thick sweeps of muscles outlining his back and the twin swells of his firm buttocks, again noticing that faint spatter of darker skin coloration. Was it freckles or something else?

Damning her curiosity which had led her so far astray this evening, Teah stopped looking at him and instead scrambled for her clothes which were scattered in a wide swath on the floor. Despite her best efforts, she couldn't find her panties, and in a whirl of near panic, decided to forget them and cover up as best she could immediately, all to facilitate her speedy exit. No one would know she wasn't wearing anything under her thick sweater and sturdy leggings. Her socks went on twisted with an uncomfortable bulge under her toes, but she didn't stop to adjust them before scuttling from the bedroom and trotting down the hallway.

She entered the large living area, determined not to slow and study the furnishings or artwork, and instead made her way to the door where her boots awaited. The kitchen was littered with the remains of the meal they hadn't shared, and her stomach twisted in a weird combination of hunger and anxiety.

Deciding dwelling on the situation was fruitless, she stepped into her boots and reached for her slicker, the idea of escape giving her some energy. Just as she touched the waterproof fabric, the front door opened and she let out a startled squeak. It opened in a smooth pivot, and she found herself face to face with Eidan's sister. The other woman grinned widely.

"Leaving so soon?"

Teah nodded, willing her face to remain placid and not flare with sudden hot embarrassment.

Brida stepped inside and quickly shed her wet coat, momentarily blocking Teah's exit as the other woman kicked out of her boots. The deputy glanced around the living space before she turned to face Teah, a slight line between her fine auburn eyebrows.

"Where's Eidan?"

Teah's mouth fell open. Well, she couldn't dissemble the obvious. "He's not here, exactly."

Brida's face settled into serious lines. "Where is he, *exactly*?"

"Ah, sleeping. In his bed." Teah was sure the other woman would be able to read between the lines and judging by the rose flush that spread up Brida's smooth cheeks, she had accurately guessed what had transpired. A slight ache twinged through Teah's pussy as she tried to forget.

"Oh! That's great, I mean, I understand. Ah … why are you leaving?"

A brief, irrelevant thought crossed Teah's mind as she shuffled around the Eleoni woman who was now studying her with a slight smile on her full lips. Were the Cozad siblings unique in their persistent questions, or did all Eleoni crave data so persistently?

"I feel it's time for me to go."

"But it doesn't even look like you had dinner," Brida said, her eyes alight with some spark of mischief.

"Yes, well, it still requires some assembly and I'm not much of a cook." Teah made a helpless gesture at the kitchen strewn with dishes and containers of vegetables, spices, and grains. "So I'll just be going—"

"Let me wake up Eidan and he can finish what he started. I'm very hungry. Long shift, you know." The other woman trotted toward the corridor containing the bedrooms, and Teah took the opportunity to flee out the door. She stifled her momentary urge to call out a polite farewell and instead plunged into the pouring rain, relief at making her escape filling her with a slightly lighter spirit.

She reached the opposite side of the street and stopped, looking back at the new modular house with regret as she adjusted her rain gear. Brida would have a bad impression of her now. Perhaps as bad as the one she had for herself.

"Hey, lookie, it's our pretty little mail girl." A loud male voice rang out, and Teah whirled to locate the speaker. She found three men sheltering under an overhang, leaning against the building behind them as if they planned to hold it up all night. It was too dark to make out their features. Her only impression was of layers of clothing covering big bodies. "And she's just crept out of the cat house after a nice long visit."

"What were you doing in there? Petting the pussy?"

Another one snorted out a greasy laugh. "Having her pussy petted more like it."

Shocked by the crudity and frightened to be alone with such boors, Teah shuffled backward, feeling for the edge of a walkway with her boot heel. Two of the men giggled and poked each other in the ribs like they'd accomplished something admirable instead of merely harassing.

"Did the sister catch you with the sheriff's dick out? Is that why you're running scared? I hope you bothered to suck him off. Otherwise he'll have to ram it somewhere else."

"Maybe his sister is taking care of it now." The one on the left gave a comical shiver, and all three laughed with foul glee.

Teah swallowed hard against the fear rushing up from her belly to lodge in her throat. This was awful, and could turn dangerous any second. Her heel clunked into a resin board, and she hoisted herself up on the walk, out of the muddy street.

The man in the middle stepped forward, and a weak beam of light brushed his face. It was one of the men from the security station, who'd brought the package Eidan had given her to deliver. One of Bokum's minions, clearly stationed here to monitor the Eleoni.

"You listen, little Collective stooge, stay out of this. It's no concern of yours." The threat was clear in the rough tone of his gravelly voice, and she found herself nodding once, doing whatever it took to placate them until she'd reached a safe distance. "And a word of advice, stay out of Eleoni beds. No decent man will want you if he finds out you've let an alien fuck you."

"That's right, it's bestality, you know." The one on the right asserted, then looked at his companions. "That's the word, right? Bestamality?"

"Animal fucker," the one in the middle stated in a flat voice. "Pity, I always fancied a turn on you, but wouldn't come near you now."

"She's probably already crawling with alien diseases," the one on the left hissed as he crossed his arms. "Disgusting."

Teah wanted to shout at them that she'd rather die than have any of them touch her, that Eidan Cozad was twice the man they'd ever be and more well-endowed than any human male, but she sucked in her outrage in favor of silence and retreat.

Backing down the walkway, she kept her eyes on her tormentors, but they didn't move from their post. As soon as she'd put several more meters between them, she spun and ran, chased by their sudden laughter all the way to the corner where she could finally disappear from their sight. The tears came then, fear, regret, and self-doubt all collided inside and jettisoned out in loud sobs and shaking hands as she stumbled toward the quiet haven of her home.

****

Eidan's head ached like someone had struck his temples repeatedly with a large mallet. He didn't want to be walking a patrol with Brida through the mucky streets of this wretched backwater. He didn't want to police this motley collection of humans who could barely make eye contact with him. He most especially didn't want to see Teah ever again. The woman had to have a mental problem. There was no other way to account for her bizarre actions of two evenings past.

A large Kotze eased past them, almost bumping him and his sister with a wobbling coil of articulated hose, and Eidan sent a surly scowl at the miner's retreating back.

"Ease back there, Sheriff. You looked like you were ready to cuff him and book him for intent to murder."

His sister's rebuke annoyed him even farther, and he shot her a quelling glare. Brida responded by quirking up her lips and shaking her head once.

"I don't know what's crawled up your exhaust vent. You've been a bundle of bad energy for days."

Eidan didn't reply to her taunt. He remembered all too well the knowing looks and teasing comments his sister had flung his way after waking him the night he and Teah had … done something he didn't care to remember because it made his head ache even worse than it already did. He still couldn't believe he'd simply fallen asleep after having sex with her. Almost as unbelievable was the fact that Teah hadn't been there when he'd woken. And she hadn't made contact since.

As if she'd read his mind, Brida spoke up. "Mind if we swing by the post office? I got a notice that a package came in for me."

"You go ahead." He reconnoitered their surroundings and realized they were only a few doors away from Teah's territory. His headache must be worse than he'd thought if he'd been that unaware of their location. Perhaps it was time to relent and take a pain reliever before he put Brida and himself at risk for lack of spatial awareness.

"Come with me. What are you going to do, stand outside and glare at people?"

"That's my job, after all."

"The glare is optional," Brida chided him. "The citizenry already resent us, so it wouldn't hurt to try being a bit more accessible. Come in the post office and chat with whoever is waiting in line. I think you'd be safe in assuming we won't have to arrest anyone in there so you can let your guard down for a few minutes."

Letting his guard down was the last thing he should be doing around Teah. He had before, and what had it gotten him? A far too rushed sexual experience followed by silent rejection.

Brida inclined her head toward the now visible post office, its yellow siding a beacon of cheerful cleanliness in the greyish muck and spattered buildings around them. Determined to resist, Eidan nevertheless found himself striding through the doors and stopping obediently to shed his dirty boots once he was inside. He was there to make his presence known to whomever was lingering. The location of the postal manager had no bearing on his actions. He certainly wasn't avoiding her. He was just damned busy.

There were two humans and a Kotze in line, and Brida obediently took her place behind the last. Eidan wandered to the side and leaned against the wall near some lockers where he could easily survey both the entrance and the counter. No one was there, and a momentary chill of concern filled him. It dispersed with a wave of prickling heat when Teah bustled through the door to the back room, her arms straining underneath a large resin shipping case. A stab of pain lanced through his brain, and he couldn't stop the wince that followed, or miss it when she saw him and stumbled.

Within a second she was focused on her customer, conducting the scanning and transfer of the package with cheerful competence even as a red flush bloomed on her cheeks. Teah soon had conducted her business with the other human customer and then began to deal with the massive Kotze. The alien miner shifted on his huge feet and mumbled out his request so quietly Teah had to ask him to repeat himself before she could collect his package. As she turned and headed back toward the storage room, she met his gaze for a hot instant. The frown she gave him triggered his already fragile temper, and he had to restrain his urge to leap over the counter and follow her, to capture her and demand she explain why she was avoiding him, why she wasn't seeking him out. He ground his teeth together instead.

Teah returned with a tiny shipping tube that looked absurd when clutched in the grateful Kotze's huge hands. The alien dipped his head and repeatedly thanked Teah like she'd gone into orbit to retrieve the thing, and Eidan's blood pressure mounted with every sweet smile she gave the man.

Finally the miner said farewell and lumbered toward the door where he slowly resumed his spiked boots, all while shooting yearning glances Teah's way. Brida, in the meantime, had made her way to the counter and greeted Teah cheerfully. Without hesitation, Teah whirled and again disappeared into the back room, this time not even looking his way.

His sister leaned her hip against the counter and folded her arms.

"Aren't you even going to say hello to her?" she hissed.

"Who?"

"Don't be obtuse. Say hello to Teah when she comes back."

"Why?"

"Because—"

Teah's return interrupted whatever plea his sister was planning, and Eidan wished he could stare at the ceiling instead of watch Teah as she happily handed over a sizeable vacu-formed cube over to Brida. His sister declared she couldn't wait to open it since it was full of new waterproof clothes, prompting Teah to quiz her on where she'd purchased them.

"You should come over and see them, try some on if you like," Brida said with a pleased lilt in her voice. Teah demurred, her eyelids fluttering down to half-conceal her deep brown eyes. Eidan wanted to punch something.

The door rattled behind them, and another miner lumbered in, shyly shifting his gaze to Teah. Blast, was every male Kotze on the planet infatuated with her?

Without waiting for his sister, he made his way to the door, stepping awkwardly around the shuffling miner in order to reach his footgear. Damn this planet, damn its weather, and damn all the circumstances that had brought him here. His peripheral vision clouded as anger brewed in his veins. With a heave he flung open the door and stepped out onto the slippery walkway, its surface coated with a layer of mud that matched the roadway just beyond. Cool, humid air hit his exposed skin, and he tried to suck in a deep, calming breath. It didn't work.

The door rattled behind him, and Brida emerged, her package shoved under her arm and a scowl on her face. Without hesitation, Eidan commenced walking, intent on returning to the security station and immersing himself in designing a new quarterly report system.

"What's wrong with you? Why didn't you even say hello to Teah?"

"She was busy."

Brida scoffed and shifted her package. "You're unbelievable. Yes, Eidan, she's so very busy her ears stopped working."

His sister's sarcastic tone whetted his ill temper even more, and he suddenly decided to assign her the task of marking all the station furnishings with property stamps.

"You don't make it easy for me to make friends when you behave so rudely."

Her words pierced the negativity that followed him like a raincloud, and he glanced over at her to find Brida frowning as she watched her step.

"I didn't realize you liked her."

"Well, I do, so stop being such an arse. I thought you liked her, too."

Eidan squinted down the thoroughfare, pretending he could see through the mist. He hadn't really considered it. He had desired Teah, desired her still despite her bizarre behavior, but did he *like* her? A rush of memory washed over him as he recalled her kindness toward her odd foundling, how determined she was to keep her workplace and person tidy and conform to regulation, the way she refused to be cowed when he tried to impose his ideas. When he considered how hard she must have worked to escape her upbringing, he realized how much he admired her.

With a shake of his head he tried to dismiss the thought. She'd rejected him, had snuck away like she was ashamed of what they'd done, so no, he couldn't admire her after all.

Brida misinterpreted his gesture. "You don't like her? But I thought you two had—"

"No." His denial was more a means to head off his sister deciding to broadcast his sexual activity to everyone passing by at the moment. The station was just ahead, and the idea of losing himself in those quarterly reports beckoned. Far better to move numbers around than remember how Teah had shuddered in his arms, how her little moans vibrated into his ear in an erotic buzz so strong he still heard it every sleepless night. He wanted to forget the fact that he'd hidden the undergarment she'd left behind deep in a drawer of his own clothing, or that he had to constantly restrain himself from seeking it out and holding it as a tangible reminder.

Brida stopped in her tracks, heedless of the people passing around her. "So what happened? Why are you avoiding her?"

"I'm not avoiding anything, Brida, and this isn't the place to discuss such matters, understood?"

Eidan eyed a trio of shabby men ambling their way, mindful of the surprise attack he and his sister had averted a few days prior. These three didn't meet his gaze as he stared and shuffled past as quickly as they could. No threat. A fresh spike of pain shattered through his head, and he tightened his jaw.

Brida sighed and gave him a sidelong look, obviously frustrated by her sibling's uncooperative behavior. "Understood."

Chapter Six

Broose circled her head, his tentacles tangling in her hair, his air jet making little whooshes of agitation. He wanted out for the night, and Teah was reluctant to release him into the dark, worried about the dangers he'd encounter on his own. The aircuttle's big black eyes rolled at the door with every circuit, and she knew she had to give in. She'd been releasing him for several weeks, and the intervals of freedom had grown longer and longer, indicating he was maturing and nearing the time where he could be independent.

Sighing out her defeat, she went to the door, and as soon as her hand hovered near the release, Broose fluttered past her face, his color fluctuating between the vivid yellow of excitement and pale orange he usually adopted when he was outside. She keyed the door open, and he swept by her in a rush, doubling back quickly to give her one quick caress with four tentacles, then jetting up into the black sky, out of her sight in the time it took for her to crane her head upwards. The movement aggravated the low headache she'd been suffering for several days. She was also running a slight fever and resolved to visit the clinic in the morning if she wasn't improved by then.

She waited a moment on the landing, hoping he might return. The town was lit for the evening with its usual assortment of inadequate and mismatched lights. She could see parts of the next street containing the majority of the entertainments Rusk offered, and had no inclination to wander over and see what mischief might be afoot. The fire at the Last Chance hadn't stopped the establishment from reopening the next day, the holes covered by tacked-on tarpaulins. She had a feeling those would remain forever in lieu of more permanent repairs, much to the dismay of Dorian.

A tiny flare of light from across the street caught her eye, and she peered at the humanoid form barely visible in the shadows. Someone was standing next to a post holding up a broken overhang. A small light flared again, and she saw a faint puff of smoke rise up from the region of the watcher's head.

She narrowed her eyes and took a step back, ready to bolt into her apartment and shut the door at the first sign of a threat. Could Bokum have sent one of his men here? The figure moved slightly, and with just that hint, she realized it was Eidan. A prickle of awareness tickled her back, and she shivered.

"I can see you." Her challenge surprised her.

The dark form shifted again, and Eidan emerged into the light far enough that she could read his impassive expression.

"Why do you release that creature at night? Isn't it dangerous?"

Teah wondered if he'd been watching her apartment before this evening. The thought didn't make her nervous as it should, but rather intrigued her.

"Aircuttles hunt at night. Broose is growing up and needs the practice."

Eidan nodded once, as if he gave his approval to her strategy, and a sudden bolt of irritation flared through her now tightened chest. She repressed a childish urge to tell him how she cared for her pet was none of his business, sheriff or not.

"Good night—"

Her attempt to exit and retreat behind her door to renew her self-castigation over their sexual escapade was interrupted by Eidan's deep voice.

"Why did you leave?"

"When? What?" Her momentary confusion made her pause at the door.

"That night. Why did you—" He stepped into the roadway, and she could see a lit pipe in his hand, the bowl emitting a trail of smoke.

"I'm not discussing that with you out here, where anyone could overhear." She had a sudden recollection of the horrible things those men had said, how frightened and powerless they'd made her feel. She shrank back against the door.

Eidan tilted his head and walked to her steps, then stomped up, his pipe now clenched between his teeth. Gathering her courage, Teah placed on hand on the siding, the other gripping the rail in her best attempt to block him.

He reached the final step and peered into her eyes. She could smell the sweet fruitiness of whatever he was smoking, could make out the slight wave in his long auburn hair, and she tried to suppress the quaver of unwelcome arousal that heated her pussy. It wasn't fair that mere proximity to him made her melt inside, but it was essential she not let it show.

"Invite me in."

"Why should I?"

He raised one boot and placed it on the top step, aligning it with her own slippered foot. He inclined his body closer as his gaze bored into hers, no hints of whatever emotion or motivation was circling in his brain was revealed on his carefully held face. She stood her ground, but it was difficult not to sway, not to lean into his hard body and wrap her arms around him again. People would see, people would judge.

"Because I'm going to find out the truth, either out here or in there. I've waited long enough."

"You've waited?" Teah knew her voice wavered up with outrage, but she couldn't hold back her reaction. "I don't owe you anything."

"I'll deal with you either here or there."

"I don't need to be dealt with—"

He brought his face close enough that she could almost feel the heat of his skin. Something dark flared in his eyes, and she was transfixed. He was going to do whatever he wanted. Her nerves thrummed, and she let out a tiny gasp as her clit swelled.

"You do. Go inside."

She wanted to defy him, to slam her door in his face and leave him in the cold, but her will failed, fading away as her breath went shallow and her limbs lost strength. Not quite sure why she was doing it, she stumbled back, her hand scrabbling for the door release. As it clicked open, Eidan narrowed his eyes and crowded up the landing, effectively herding her back into her small apartment. Before she realized quite what had happened, he was inside and shutting the door, sealing them in for the confrontation to come.

"Were you watching me?"

"Only when you came outside." His laconic reply didn't match the tension she saw in his shoulders or the way his mouth tightened after every word.

"Why?"

"Because I needed to know. I need to know why."

She shook her head slowly, helpless at discovering his meaning. As if he disliked her momentary silence, he reached out to capture her elbow in one of his big hands. She almost flinched, the intensity of his expression making her think he'd squeeze too tight, but instead he was gentle, his fingers barely pressing against the fabric covering her skin.

"Why did you leave me?"

His question knocked her guard down, and she drew in a surprised breath. "I … you fell asleep, and I was cold. You were ignoring me, and I decided to go." She resolved not to tell him about the humiliating encounters that had followed.

He frowned and shook his head once, his hand still cupping her elbow. "You should have stayed. There were blankets, and I would have warmed you. I wasn't ignoring you, but was simply exhausted."

That was all true. Her excuse was unmasked as petty and inappropriate. She drew in a shaky breath. "I'm sorry for assuming you didn't want me there. It says more about me than you that I decided we didn't need to pretend any sort of connection between us."

At that, his grip tightened slightly. "No connection? Is that a human turn of phrase implying you don't want anything to do with me? Is that why you didn't come to me?"

Teah shook her head compulsively, not quite sure what she was denying. "No, what I meant was we aren't … we don't owe each other anything."

Eidan's face settled into a ferocious frown, and she stumbled a step back, restrained by his hand circling her arm. "Why not?"

His question came out in an intimidating low growl, and for the first time that evening, Teah saw him as an Eleoni. A flicker of caution worked its way along her nerves. She'd seen him beat another man with clinical precision, knew he and his sister had handily defeated Bokum's enforcers at Henderson's restaurant. Would he…

"Why are you shivering?"

His barked question made her start with fright, and she was ashamed to find incipient tears burning her eyelids. Were those men right? Doing something so intimate with a man from an entirely different culture had been a foolish blunder. She'd never understand Eidan's thoughts or motivations.

"Answer me."

"Stop demanding!" Teah flinched at the panicked tone in her voice and pressed her trembling lips together. Eidan paused and surveyed her, obviously taking in his hand on her arm, her hunched shoulders, the way her body was shaking with nerves and emotion. He slowly removed his hand and then held both palms up, fingers wide-spread.

"I'm sorry I fell asleep."

She nodded once to show she accepted his apology, not trusting her voice any longer.

"I'm sorry my questions disturb you. I'm merely trying to understand our interaction."

"I'm completely confused." Her thoughts were as tangled as a neglected skein of yarn. "I'm not sure what to do. We're so different."

Eidan eased out a long breath and watched her silently. The moments between them stretched out as Teah urged her shoulders to relax, her heart to slow. He hadn't done anything to trigger any sort of fear on her part. She'd allowed her own conflicted emotions to rocket her into an upset orbit.

"I want to talk with you. So we learn about each other."

His request, accompanied by a softening of his stern features, eased her anxiety. Did she want him to remain or leave?

"Now?"

He nodded and glanced past her at her small sofa. A little shiver went through her. Anticipation or dread? Her uncertainty about him and the reactions he triggered in her nearly paralyzed her.

"All right. Would you like something to drink?"

****

Eidan took a seat on her little yellow sofa and watched Teah bustle around in her kitchen. Her living space was so small he could see all of it, other than the bath and bedroom he assumed was located behind a closed door. Considering the bed surely lurking nearby had his thoughts racing toward the idea of getting her naked again. They'd brokered a slight peace between them, and he couldn't help but want to regain that same intimacy with her. His skin heated and his blood raced as he watched her bend over to retrieve a bottle from a lower cabinet. He'd had his hands on those full mounds of flesh and desired to do so again, as soon as possible. She'd be beautiful on all fours in front of him, her full pussy raised for his attentions.

She returned with two glasses filled with a clear liquid he discovered was water as soon as he sipped it. A basic offering, the bare minimum for hospitality. It seemed he'd have to make an effort to convince her to welcome him into her body again.

After a slight hesitation, she settled next to him, her deep brown eyes searching his face while a slight blush warmed her cheeks. He longed to slide his hand between her thighs and press his palm to her sex. It would be warm and soft and she would sigh and lie back as her eyelids fluttered. His heat rate accelerated.

"What did you want to talk about?"

Eidan hesitated a moment, sure if he blurted out his desire to lick her to a noisy climax, she'd bolt from her seat in a shocked rush. Best hear her explanation of the question that had burned inside him since that evening he'd woken to find her gone and an ache tightening his temples. With a blink he realized for the first time since that night, he was free of pain. He was lightheaded, but beyond that, felt like himself. "I'd like to know why you didn't see me the next morning."

She blinked and tightened her lips. "You could have contacted me."

A deflection. "You left first."

And there it was, as close to an admission of his hurt at her rejection as he was prepared to make.

She shifted her seat and looked down at the hands she had clasped in her lap, one loosened strand of bronzy hair escaping the pins holding the rest in place. Broose had probably disarranged it before he'd flown free.

"Would you have even wanted me to stay?" Her question was so soft he leaned forward to catch the last whispered syllables.

"Yes." He hoped his sincerity came through. Why would she think he wouldn't want her there? He wanted her, both for sexual pleasure and because he was interested in her as a person. Were humans really that different in their needs?

She glanced up then, her eyes bright as she considered him. She was close enough to kiss, close enough to touch and he wanted to do both with a force that shook him to his bones. "I should have called you, shouldn't I?"

"Yes. We could have had this conversation before this misunderstanding ate away at both of us."

Teah dropped her gaze and clasped her hands together. "What else do you want to talk about?"

Her abrupt segue confused him for a moment, and when he saw the slight smile curving her mouth he knew she'd meant it to. Trust his spirited human to think she should take control of the conversation.

"Do you feel any particular animus towards me?"

She took a sip of water and then slowly shook her head. "No, not beyond how annoying your incessant questioning can become."

Again she smiled, more broadly this time, and he was heartened that she'd softened her criticism and seemed to be relaxing into his company yet again. "I should ask the same. Are you angry with me? Will you call Brida to arrest me after this interrogation?"

He wanted her far away from the security station, away from the weapons and implied violence of his profession. Locking her up somewhere safe, somewhere only he could find, was an attractive prospect. The more time he spent in Rusk amongst its amoral ruffians, the more concerned he grew for her safety.

"Normally I question a suspect or witness under much more uncomfortable circumstances."

"You mean you confine them in a tiny room with no windows, a hard seat, and bright lights?" The teasing lilt was back in her voice, and he relished in it.

"Exactly. Do you happen to have such a location on the premises?"

Her expression shifted from amused to serious. He wondered momentarily if his attempts to tease back had fallen flat, yet another incidence of cultural misunderstanding that seemed to make such a detrimental impact on their interactions.

The tip of her tongue emerged to stroke her full lower lip and his cock throbbed. "There's only my bedroom, but I just have a bed in there, and a small light. It's cozy, not intimidating."

Eidan told himself to calm down, to not grab at her legs and pull her astride him so he could finally gain access to those full breasts he knew were hiding underneath her loose tunic. So instead of laying his hands on her hips, her waist, her ass like he'd wanted to do since the first time she'd defied him, he instead reached out and slid his fingers along hers. She flinched slightly but didn't pull away. She curved her palm up, and he took the opportunity to stroke it, then the soft skin of her wrist. He could hear her breathing in the quiet of the apartment and was gratified to detect a slight irregularity.

"Is your hand better?"

"Yes. Thank you for asking."

Her shoulders slumped slightly, and she leaned his way almost imperceptibly. If he wasn't paying such close attention, if he wasn't so attuned to her and the possibilities that rose between them, he would have missed it.

"Kiss me," he said in a low voice and her hand shivered in his.

"No."

"Why not?"

"I've always kissed you first."

A fair point. His body fairly hummed as he leaned close. She stared at him for a long second, and her eyes closed. Her scent filled his consciousness as he sank into her warmth, finding her full lips as soft as before. He gripped his hand into her hair and tugged on her hand, then her legs, pulling her across his lap and leaning her down as he increased the pressure against her still closed mouth.

"Open to me," he growled, too anxious to gain more stimulation to seduce her more gently.

"All these orders make me stubborn." She hardly felt uncooperative with her warm weight sprawled across his lap, blinking up at him and twining her arms around his shoulders.

"We should be very precise in our communication to avert any potential misadventures."

She grinned in a lopsided manner. "In that case, what, exactly to you want me to open?"

"Your mouth." As soon as she complied, he returned to kissing her, taking the opportunity to suck at her lips, tease her tongue, and encourage her to so the same to him. His muscles tightened, and he gathered her closer, needing to feel her against him as completely as was possible. Faint moans escaped Teah's throat whenever he drew back, and he finally stopped long enough to catch his breath. Her thighs trembled atop his legs as she panted. Energy and determination filled him. They would have intercourse very soon, he was sure.

"Open your legs."

Her swollen lips began to form a "why", but he narrowed his eyes, daring her to argue. Some other time he'd debate her, seduce her, engage in a playful tease, but now his need was too great to rein in. His cock was so engorged it hurt, and he had to find release deep in her body or be in agony. With a little sigh, she complied, allowing one leg to fall to the side as he leaned over her. Still holding her unfocused gaze with his own, he slid his hand up her inner thigh until he could press his hand to her pussy, the sudden heat of her plump sex burning her desire into his skin.

She shivered and jerked, clutching at his shoulders even as he kissed her again, working slower this time and allowing his fingers to stroke a rhythm along the folds he could make out through the thin fabric of her garment. Soon enough, she'd dampened the material and her rich scent filled the air, beckoning and beguiling him.

He remembered how she'd come to climax so quickly before, and rather than again manually stroke her to pleasure, he instead wished for a more intimate caress. He shifted his position on the sofa to ease the pressure on his swollen cock and to allow him better access between her legs. With a few quick tugs, he removed her lower garment to find her bare beneath. Her creamy thighs spread wide, revealing the damp curls between her legs that provocatively framed the full, pink lips of her slick pussy. He thought he could make out the tight nub of her clit nearly hidden in a feminine whorl of flesh, but the only way to be sure was to explore.

He lowered his head and pressed his mouth to her, taking in her moisture and tangy flavor with relief. She tasted just right, and all the slippery puckers of flesh he licked enticed him to caress, suck, and nibble every succulent millimeter of her. Her body jerked under his hands, and he caught her in a restraining grasp at her full hips. He tongued first one side, then the other of her rigid clit, discovering the best sequence of movements as Teah squealed and shuddered. Within what seemed like too few moments, she was gasping out his name and digging her fingers into his hair, pulling it free of its restraints as she bucked.

A strained cry left her as she convulsed again and again, her legs thrashing in erratic spasms as her pleasure released. Eidan slowed his movements, merely resting his tongue against her twitching clit as he looked up her body to see her head rocking back and forth as she struggled for breath. She'd pulled up her tunic and was cupping her breast and pinching her nipple so tightly it poked between her fingertips. Her abandon was beautiful. Such a delicious treat to please her so thoroughly.

****

Completely exposed. Teah took what she hoped was a controlling breath and willed herself back to reality. Aftershocks of unrivaled orgasms still pulsed along her nerves and tingled in her muscles, but she drew herself together well enough to glance down her body to find

Eidan lodged between her legs, staring up, his mouth still damp from her. His eyes were dark purple, and the intensity of his gaze made her clit pulse with renewed need. Not that she could come again, it would be impossible for any sort of renewal on her part. She'd need several days to recover from that experience.

He squeezed her hips in his hands once, then rose and looked down at her as she tried to bring her uncooperative legs together, to muster some sort of control over her shivering body and thudding heart. She pulled down her blouse, covering the breast she'd caressed as he'd suckled her clit. He reached out and nudged her hand up under the material again, and she automatically cupped herself. He gave a slight nod, and as she stroked her still sensitized skin, she grasped her other, ignored-'til-now breast and flicked the hard nipple with her thumbnail. Petite jolts of sensation flared out from each puckered twist of flesh, and she couldn't hold back a little moan of dark delight. Having his gaze on her made it all the more stimulating. Something about him transformed her and she relaxed into her wantonness. Let them talk. This man thrilled her.

"I want you to go to the bedroom." He rumbled out the request, not quite ordering, but still decisive enough that the pliant part of herself she'd never listened to before had her on her unsteady feet and moving. She wondered what Eidan thought of her wobbling ass, her full thighs, but as she entered the dark bedroom and he demanded light from the wall unit, she understood he liked what he saw. Somehow, her satiated pussy warmed and swelled anew.

He reached for the hem of her tunic and pulled it off over her head, leaving her completely bare while he was clothed from neck to ankles. It didn't matter any longer. Her body was his prize, and she surrendered to his need. His hands skated along her sides, nearly tickling her sensitive ribs until they settled at her breasts, supporting their weight as he leaned close and rubbed his beard on her cheek and neck. It was a stunning reminder of how he'd tickled her inner thighs just minutes before as he'd so softly drawn his tongue against her clit.

"Do I touch you as well as you touch yourself?" His soft question was accompanied by twin tugs against her erect nipples, the prior gentle pleasure she'd given herself intensified enough now to make her gasp and grow wet.

"Yes."

His hand crept up over her breast, brushing past her collarbone as he finally spread his fingers alongside her neck, teasing at her pinned hair. Guessing his desire, she reached up to loosen all the twists and tangles, keeping her pins tight against her palm at she removed each one. After a few snarls and struggles, it was down, warm and silky as it brushed the skin of her shoulders and upper back. He made a low sound of approval and rubbed at her nipple. Her knees weakened, and she staggered.

"You need to be on the bed before you fall. Face the headboard and stay on your knees."

His cool demand made her shiver with hot arousal. Yes, she would do this because it was going to be wonderful. Teah moved to comply, losing sight of him immediately as she turned and crawled across the bed, discarding the hairpins heedlessly on the sheet. Face to her plain upholstered headboard, she felt the bed shift and dip as he followed her. His broad hands caressed her thighs, her ass cheeks, and finally gripped at her hanging breasts. Her skin pricked with each anticipated stroke, and a little groan left her as he again pinched at her nipples. She felt the fabric of his clothing brushing against the backs of her thighs and momentarily wondered why he was still dressed. His knee pressed to hers to encourage her to widen them further and she complied.

He drew away again, rubbing along her back and cupping her hips until she tilted them, and she glanced over her shoulder to see what he was doing. Eidan knelt behind her, his gaze riveted to her exposed pussy. Awareness that he was staring at her most private flesh, now wet and swelling again just from his nearness, made her flinch and try to draw her knees closer. He quickly slid his hands up her inner thighs and held them apart. Her clit pulsed, and a small, agitated voice in her head pleaded with him to run his fingers against that throbbing bit of flesh, to slide a thick finger inside her up to the final knuckle. He did neither of those things.

Eidan inclined his head to one side and pressed a wet kiss to one of her ass cheeks. She jolted at the unanticipated contact, and jolted again when he bit down softly on her tender flesh. She couldn't hold back an agonized whine, and closed her eyes tight, falling in to herself as all her awareness centered on the warm, wet caresses he was giving her. She didn't talk, didn't wonder why or what he thought, but instead concentrated on his tongue, his teeth, his warm breath centered on flesh that had never experienced such attention.

She shuddered again when he slid two fingers up and down her slit, the slick sound of her body and his movement seeming to echo in the quiet room. Slow strokes, some of which circled her opening, spread her tingling folds, others that framed her swollen clit, all brought her to a panting agony.

"Please," she begged, arching her back and inclining her hips in as clear an invitation as she'd ever given. His hands retreated, and she screwed her eyes up even tighter and bit her lip.

There was the soft swish of fabric moving, a metallic clink, and then the warmth of him pressing close behind. His fingers rubbed lightly at her opening, then eased her wider for the press of his wide, smooth cock head. He pushed in, not nearly fast enough, and her legs trembled with the strain of waiting. More and more of his hard cock filled her, and she exhaled, trying to relax some of the incredible tension filling her so his way was easier. His harsh breathing accelerated as soon as he was fully encased within her. One of his hands slid up her back and threaded through the hair hanging in a loose hank at the back of her neck as the other cupped around her stomach, two fingertips squeezing either side of her aching clit.

"Hold steady for me, *alati*," he gasped, and she locked her knees and elbows. The first bold thrust nearly sent her toppling into the headboard, and she shifted one hand to press against its firm surface as he pulled back his hips and pushed home again. "That's right. Hold me tight."

His rough-voiced encouragement energized her, and she rocked her hips to coincide with his movements, not even thinking of her own arousal, only wanting to give him the most erotic sensation she could. She managed several coordinated movements, but lost all focus when he began to flick two fingertips across the edge of her throbbing clit. Eidan's thrusts increased in tempo, and he groaned out loud with each. Unable to draw a deep breath or move her head against the firm grip he had in her hair, Teah gave herself up, waves of pleasure slamming through her as he worked himself deep inside.

With a howling grunt, he shuddered against her, his cock pulsing against her tight sheath. A gasping sigh of pleasure and triumph burst from her as he stroked in and out a few more times, then curled around her, drawing her back against his legs as they half sat in the bed. She wrenched her eyes open and looked down to see his reddish, wide cock still buried between her bright pink and slick lips. Drawing in a shuddering breath, she brushed her fingertips along the strained flesh where they were still joined, easily sliding from hers to his and back again.

Eidan heaved out huge breaths and tightened his arms around her. "You aren't going anywhere."

"I know, I live here," she managed to whisper, regretting the loss of pressure as his softening cock slid from her. A rush of fluids escaped her and trickled down her thighs. Eidan's chest hair tickled her back as he moved her slightly, and then he kissed her shoulder and neck.

With a deep sigh, he reclined to his side, pulling her along with him. The flesh he'd nipped stung slightly as she moved. She allowed herself to relax and enjoy the secure feeling of being held in his strong arms. Time enough to consider her actions later, when she wasn't so lightheaded and satiated.

****

Teah's hair was longer than his, but not by much. Eidan was contentedly brushing out the final section, enjoying the way the strands shone and mingled with each other in a smooth wave of honey-brown. He also liked looking at her petite shoulders and delicate backbone as it curved down to her full ass. The dimples above either succulent cheek were especially delightful. It was strange to touch a woman free of glauca, but he liked the expanse of her unmarked skin nevertheless.

A few pink crescents denting her ass revealed where he'd indulged himself earlier, and he was already anticipating their next time. He hadn't given any attention to her sweet little rear hole, and he had a feeling, based on how she'd leaned into his bites, that some play and penetration of that small opening would be appreciated, both by her and him.

It was pleasant to count on the next time. Teah showed no signs of wanting him to leave her bed, and he had hopes she'd soon invite him under her coverings for the night. But first he had to attend to her hair. He'd tangled it quite badly when he'd held her in position, and he wasn't the sort of man to leave his woman in disarray. She'd insisted on cleaning away the swirls of his seed and her own delicious juices, but the next time he'd be sure to care for her there.

"What does *alati* mean?" Teah glanced over her shoulder and slanted an inquiring look his way.

"Where did you hear that?"

"You called me that twice before. Tonight when you first mounted me, and another time, before we kissed."

He didn't recall even speaking at such an intense moment. It was a fitting appellation for her. "It's Eleoni for guardian spirit. A mythical creature who flies and watches over children."

"Like an angel?"

Eidan shuffled through his knowledge of human legends. "Yes, very similar. *Alati* are a bit more formidable. They carry flaming tridents to pierce the eyes of evildoers."

She huffed out a laugh. "You picture me with a flaming pitchfork?"

"Not specifically."

She turned her head and gave him an inquiring look as she glanced at his chest and arms. He gently turned her back around so he could continue his work.

"What are those marks on your body called? Those spots? They aren't freckles because they're too regular."

It was a natural question considering her skin was clear, with nary a flaw, other than the ones he'd just bestowed. "Eleoni gain their glauca in adolescence, with the onset of puberty. They increase and darken until full adulthood, then remain until death."

"I can feel them when we touch." She reached back and stroked along the spray that marked his thigh to demonstrate. His skin shivered and his muscles twitched as her touch seemed to stimulate each small mark. "But before, it was too dark for me to make them out. Are they sensitive?"

Actually, his had been feeling tender, and the way his body reacted when her skin came in contact with them was unusual. "A bit."

She continued to stroke him, seeming to enjoy the sensation of the raised bumps running along her palm. A warm buzz crept through his body, and he sighed with satisfaction. She tugged his arm forward and nuzzled the line than ran from elbow to wrist. He jolted as if she'd run her tongue along his balls. Before he could ask her to repeat the motion, she released him and rolled her shoulders, clearly wishing him to continue brushing her hair. Yes, he would relish a night beside this woman, and look forward to the next. As he picked up the brush, a thought that had bothered him for some days emerged from the haze of good feeling he'd been wallowing in. "I have to apologize for another thing. I didn't complete dinner for you. Perhaps we could manage to go out and share a meal."

If they were anywhere private, he had the feeling they would indulge in sex rather than food. Not a bad exchange, but he wished companionship beyond copulation with her.

Her shoulders tightened, and she sat straighter. "That might not be such a good idea."

"I can assure you that the slight altercation that occurred at the restaurant will not be repeated."

She turned and faced him, a deep frown pulling down her soft lips. "You can't be sure of that. You know Bokum is going to try again."

He stroked his fingers across her shoulder and down her arm. She took the opportunity to fold herself against his chest, tucking her legs up over his as she circled her arms around his shoulders. This brought her breasts and belly close, and he caressed those soft mounds of flesh. "Brida would never allow it. We are well on the way to collecting evidence and soon will have him incarcerated, and his web of corruption thoroughly rooted out."

She was still frowning so he kissed her. Her mouth opened under his, and she trembled as he nibbled along her upper lip. Her nipples were already hard nubs, and he wondered if her clit was equally aroused.

"They're desperate. They'll try something unexpected, and no matter how brave and smart you are, you might be caught by surprise. Perhaps they even did something to the marshal. Who knows what sort of thing they'll use against you?" Her breathy little protest moved him, and he paused to consider that if Teah's relationship with him were known, she might be in danger. Just the thought of someone kidnapping her in order to control him, or doing something even more nefarious, filled him with cold determination to keep her safe and destroy anyone who might pose a threat to her.

"Sweet Teah, I'll keep you safe from all harm."

"I wasn't thinking of me. I'll be fine no matter what anyone says."

"Who said something?" Now thoughts of pleasure receded. If there was already talk about them, she was at risk.

She glanced away, her cheeks a deep pink. "Nothing. Just some men making crude remarks. They say mean things about everyone."

"Such as?" Eidan longed to demand a detailed account, but a more gentle interrogation was in order for his *alati*. The last thing he wanted to do was put her on the defensive, for if he did, they would argue and not share information easily. He trusted she'd tell him as best she could. She ran her fingertips along the spray of glauca that outlined his abdominals, and he sighed with pleasure.

Her lids fluttered, and he thought he detected some moisture on her lashes. "They said human women were ruined if they had intercourse with Eleoni. That anyone who…" She paused as if searching for the right word. "Anyone who was intimate with another species was no better than someone who'd have sex with an animal."

How upsetting for her. How insulting to him. "Do you see me as an animal?"

"Oh, *no*!" In a sudden flurry of movement she was holding him tightly, staring at him as a tear rolled down her cheek. "You're a man, a wonderful man who pleases me so well. You're honorable and trustworthy. And handsome."

She whispered the last and brought her mouth to his for a soft kiss, almost as if she expected for him to turn away. "Do you see *me* as alien?"

He stroked her cheek, and she spread her legs to circle around his hips. He settled to a more balanced position on the bed and pulled her tight in his lap. The springy curls between her legs rubbed his lower belly, and the warm, wet folds of her pussy aligned with his half-hard cock now swelling to life. "You are a beautiful woman. Mysterious, as some women can be, but not alien."

With a smile she relaxed. "I saw you as different, and sometimes hard to deal with, but never really as an *alien*. Just different."

He kissed her shoulder for the compliment, then nibbled along her neck. She shivered and moaned, and moisture coated his cock. Oh, his little human was needy again, and so soon. He'd see to her lovely body's desires. "I'm feeling hard to deal with at the moment. Lie back."

With a stuttering sigh she released her hold on his shoulders and leaned away from him, lowering herself to the tangled covers of her bed, her legs still wrapped around his waist. This elevated her hips and opened her to his eyes and hands. So vulnerable, so giving. With one hand he stroked up and down her torso, playing with her breasts, pinching her tight nipples, tickling her upper thighs. With the other he took his engorged cock and slid it along her pussy, coating it with her fragrant fluids, then positioning the tip against her deep pink clit peeking from a tiny knot of flesh. Her eyelids went heavy, while shallow, ragged breaths tore from her, making her breasts shake.

"Work against it, my sweet."

He held his cock steady as she slowly found a rhythm, her hips rocking. He could actually feel the hard flesh of her engorged clit as it slid along the sensitive underside of his cock. When her movements brought it in alignment with his opening, now leaking pre-cum, the sensation was so intense, yet tender, he had to suck in deep breaths so as not to spurt his seed all over her belly.

Another time he'd do that, come between her breasts, in her mouth, but not now.

Teah clutched at the bedcovers and cried out his name in a frenzied moan. With a quick movement, he pushed his cock against her opening, her hot flesh seeming to suck him in as she arched her hips. Eidan threw his head back as she took his whole length, then allowed himself the pleasure of looking down at her trembling, impaled body. She stared up at him, her eyes wide.

"Can you see?" she groaned, then spread her legs even farther apart, planting her feet on the mattress and arching back to reveal her slick pussy pierced by his thick cock, her clit now unattended. He gripped her hips and kept them tilted back, in preparation for the work to come.

"Yes, and you are a luscious dream. Touch yourself."

She slid one hand down her belly, then delved her fingers along her pussy, lubricating herself as she circled around the base of his cock, squeezing him before retreating to rest them along either side of her clit. He began to thrust, using his thigh muscles to push and his hold on her hips to move her against his cock. The wet, sucking sound that accompanied each penetration thrilled him, as did the sight of his member emerging shiny with her fluids, then burying deep inside her heat once again.

Teah thrashed as her fingers rapidly massaged her little clit. All too soon her whole body tightened and she stared wildly up at him, her mouth open as she panted. Eidan allowed his own arousal to flare and as soon as he told her to come, he did as well, his muscles shuddering with electric pulses. Jolt after jolt of near painful pleasure shot from his balls out his cock as he released deep within her. She wailed and strained as fresh fluids poured from her pussy. Her body, working so hard to welcome and please him, as hard as his body strained to fill her with his seed and open her womb with climax after climax. Perfectly compatible.

He gasped for breath and leaned forward so his cock would not slip free too soon. With hoarse murmurs, Teah ran her hands up his arms and laced her fingers behind his neck. His glauca burned at her touch.

"I think those men were right about one thing."

He was too sated to build another wave of anger against their opponents. "What is that?"

"You have ruined me for human men."

Chapter Seven

"I would have thought getting to have intercourse again would put you in a better mood. I know it would help me snap out of my foul temper." Brida grumbled as Eidan drove them to the outskirts of town as they made their way to an appointment with the planet's science station. It was located several kilometers from the settlement and the two locations were linked with a narrow, ungraded path, so he and his sister were taking one of the security vehicles to make this first, formal introduction to the scientists more expedient. His sister obviously saw their journey as an opportunity to chatter.

"I don't know what you're talking about."

She shot him a narrow-eyed look. "So, last night the sounds from your room were caused by what? A pornographic entertainment you couldn't be bothered to mute? And why would Teah be eating breakfast with you the next morning if she hadn't spent the night?"

Eidan shut his mouth, sure he didn't want to comment on anything Brida had said. Yes, Teah and he had been very vocal while having intercourse the night before. He'd introduced her to an anal plug, a tiny black one he wasn't sure why he'd even packed since it was too small stimulate him. But it had fit her untested opening perfectly and as he recalled how she'd moaned and her pussy had slicked with moisture as he'd slowly eased it in, his cock thickened. Then it had been his turn to moan when he'd mounted her and the hard knob of the plug had rubbed his cock in the perfect spot. He couldn't recall ever coming so hard in his life. He made a note to order more toys sized for her petite openings. He'd love to watch her work a dildo deep inside her sex.

"I invited her for breakfast to make up for the dinner we missed."

Brida scoffed and shook her head. "That doesn't explain why you were feeding her honey from your fingers when I walked in."

No, there was no innocent explanation for that. He wasn't going to tell Brida that episode had been Teah's idea. Following his human's suggestions when it came to seduction was turning out to be very rewarding. She'd promised to anoint select glauca with the sticky substance and lave him clean with her tongue the next time they had privacy in the kitchen. His cock ached anew, echoing the pain growing in his head.

By this time they'd left the settlement behind, and were passing an expanse of muddy soil that seemed to stretch to the horizon. This was the site of the original surface mine and it still looked like a warscape even though the Kotze miners had moved further afield in pursuit of fossilized coral balls. The spheres were loaded with rare minerals and at this point were the only resources this planet had to offer the outside galaxy.

The barrenness of the landscape was finally broken when the trail descended into the edge of an imposing stand of grasswood. Brida slowed the cart as they entered the forest-like growth. It was now difficult to see more than a few meters ahead of them, and the light was dimmed by the huge, flat spires that waved overhead. Perhaps there would be aircuttles among the looming plants.

Brida scanned the path and the trunks that crowded close, reacting to the loss of visibility as any trained professional would. Eidan would like to think there was no cause for worry, but that would be folly. Their opponents, while not especially intimidating when compared to criminals that dominated entire cities or continents on other planets, still wielded power here.

They'd gone several hundred meters into the forest when they found their way blocked by a fallen grasswood. The trunk was nearly a meter in diameter and far too large for the cart's tires to scale without the undercarriage hanging up. Eidan brought the machine to a halt as he and his sister considered the dilemma.

Just as he turned to her with the suggestion that they get out and reconnoiter a detour, Brida yelled out for him to back up. Without bothering to ask her why, he slammed the drive into reverse and accelerated away from the barrier. The forest on either side erupted with noise and the distinctive clangs and pings of projectile weapons clattered around them. Brida immediately returned fire, spraying magnetized shells in a wide arc to cover their retreat.

The plants surrounding them blurred as he pushed the cart to its limits and somehow managed to keep it on the narrow, slippery path. Brida held her fire, and he strained to hear movement or any more attempts to ambush them from their unseen assailants. The only sound was that of the cart's straining engine and the sloppy suction of the tires in the muck.

Eidan drew a deep breath and winced. An ache bloomed in his chest and he glanced down to see a dark and shiny stain spreading across his uniform tunic.

"You're hit!" Brida yelled, and he simply nodded at her, his arms weakening so rapidly he dropped the steering bar. His vision clouded, and the last thing he recognized was the unfamiliar sun whirling in the sky overhead.

****

"Did you hear?" Dorian's voice rang out from her personal comm., and Teah glanced around the deserted post office with a start, embarrassed she hadn't put it on mute.

"Hear what?"

"The Eleoni were shot in the forest, on the way to the science station."

Teah went numb. She worked her cold lips a few times before she could speak. It seemed impossible that vigilant Brida and Eidan, *Eidan*, could be hurt. "Are you sure?"

"Yep. One of my players got a call while he was at my table and he told me. Then we heard the siren when the cart came roaring through town."

She braced her elbows on the counter and lowered her head to counteract the sudden dizziness that swept through her. "Are they dead?"

"Don't see how they could have lived. From what my player told me, there were at least ten shooters involved."

Teah noticed a whining noise and wondered if sudden shock and grief could alter one's hearing. But no, there was a siren outside, wailing in the distance. Had they needed to send another cart back to rescue one of the Eleoni? Had Eidan been lying in the mud all this time?

"Dorian, I hear another siren. I have to go."

"But wait, Teah, I—"

She shut off his call and stumbled around the counter to the front door. She was going to lock the place up, in complete disregard for the posted open hours. After keying in the lock code, she broke into a trot, the shriek of the alarm leading her closer and closer to whatever emergency it signaled.

She rounded the corner to the main road and came up short. What seemed like twenty Eleoni in shiny black riot armor lined the street, huge weapons at the ready. She suddenly remembered Eidan mentioning his reinforcements arrived that afternoon. He'd been so happy. It wasn't past the noon meal, so these new officers must have heard about the attack and moved up their landing.

Clusters of wide-eyed humans stayed clear of the intimidating security forces while the few Kotze in the street went about their business.

Gathering up her courage, Teah took a breath and approached the closest Eleoni. It was a woman with bright turquoise eyes and a grim expression.

"Do you know anything about the Cozads?"

"No. Move along." The Eleoni's curt tone and hard frown put to rest any notion Teah had for an exchange of information. Making good on the order, she backed away from the line of troopers and trotted down the alley. The medical clinic was just to the south of the line of Eleoni and she could sneak past them by walking behind a row of buildings. She found the back of the clinic and made her way along the side to the walk-up pharmacy window. A nurse whom she knew from genial exchanges at the post office was inside and he gave her a nod. When Teah requested admittance, the man glanced away toward the main part of the building as if he was checking on something, then pointed toward a side door next to him. It buzzed open, and she dashed inside.

"I'm here to see the Cozads."

The nurse widened his eyes. "They're in lockdown."

Teah gulped as her stomach sank. "Are they alive?"

"I can't say, that's confidential." The expression on the nurse's face was downcast, and Teah had to assume the worst. Tears burned at her eyes and her breathing went ragged as she contemplated Eidan's lifeless body being held somewhere in this building. And Brida, poor Brida.

Tightening her trembling lips, Teah stepped past the man and slipped through another door, finding herself in a vaguely familiar corridor. If she headed to the left, she should be able to make her way to the individual treatment rooms reserved for serious cases. She'd been there a month ago to pick up Dorian after he'd recovered from a migraine. There was a babble of voices from that direction, and she hurried along, trying to look official. She passed only one other medic, who was too busy looking over a monitor to notice, and then was in the small administration room for the treatment area. It was a hive of activity with doctors and nurses talking with each other all and shuffling supplies while being monitored by two silent and armed Eleoni.

Teah glanced around and noticed a trail of blood droplets on the floor. Steeling herself, she followed the smeared and spattered line until it ended at a closed door. Either Eidan or Brida was inside.

With a hiss, the translucent panel slid back and an orderly bustled out with a cloth bag in hand. Teah peered inside and saw Brida leaning over a figure shrouded on the bed while a doctor monitored something on a nearby display. Not realizing what she was doing until she was inside, Teah rushed to Brida and grabbed her hand.

"Thank it all, you're here. My comm was destroyed in the fight, and I couldn't find Eidan's to contact you." The other woman babbled as Teah looked down at the man sprawled in the bed.

He was so still and pale. She'd never seen Eidan with anything less than tremendous presence, and to see him struck down and immobilized was almost unbelievable. His coppery hair was dark and matted as it spread across the white pillow and smears of rusty blood marred his cheek and neck. The rest of him was hidden under a sheet, and as she stared, his chest rose and fell slightly. He was alive.

"What happened?" She could barely manage the simple question. Brida clutched her hand even tighter, and even in Teah's shocked state, she was grateful for the contact.

"Ambush in the forest. We took fire from two flanks after halting at an obstacle. Eidan got us out, but he was hit in the chest. Armor-piercing." The other woman's clipped delivery failed to mask the quaver in her voice.

Teah stopped staring at Eidan's face and looked at the doctor. "Will he live?"

"You are?" The doctor gave a pointed look at the door Teah had burst through.

"She's with me. Tell her everything," Brida spat out, with a foul look for the man opposite her. The doctor inhaled and set his jaw before turning to Teah.

"He's sustained significant damage to the lungs, liver, and assorted tissue in between—"

"Not that you'd know better." Brida shot out.

The doctor, a tall man with short dark hair and vivid blue eyes, frowned. "Deputy, I assure you yet again I'm fully qualified to treat an Eleoni patient."

"I want my own medic in here. She's waiting outside—"

"She's a fine medic, I'm sure, but her training is for battlefield triage—"

"This is a battlefield wound!" Brida was shouting at this point, and Teah understood the other woman's frustration and fear, for the same emotions were drowning her from the inside. Teah squeezed Brida's hand, and she went suddenly silent, her whole body rigid.

The doctor inhaled deeply. "He's stabilized."

Teah licked her lips, her whole mouth dry as she framed the next question. "Will he survive?"

The doctor tore his gaze from Brida's and focused on her, his eyes softening a fraction. "He's strong and got here very quickly. The initial surgery went well, so I'm optimistic. Everything that could be done has been."

She sagged against the table, then drew back very quickly in fear that she might have jarred something on Eidan's prostrate form. Brida squeezed her hand in return, and she gave the other woman a grateful look.

"What can I do? How can I help?"

"He knows you're here," the doctor said, indicating a bright blue line squiggling along a monitor. "So talk with him, let him know he's going to be all right, be encouraging."

"Can I touch him?" Teah couldn't stop the pleading tone in her voice. She was desperate to make sure he was warm, detect the flicker of a pulse. Any sign that he was alive.

The doctor nodded. "Just avoid the bandaged areas. Tactile stimulation can aid the healing process."

Teah crouched down on a stool next to the bed and rested her fingertips against his forehead. Brida and the doctor engaged in a whispered confrontation that Teah tuned out. There were dark circles under Eidan's closed eyes, and now that some of the initial shock was wearing off, she noticed dried mud and blood all over his skin. "I want to clean him up."

She turned and found both the doctor and Brida staring at her like she'd spouted some inappropriate poetry. After a long moment while Teah wondered if she'd have to repeat herself, the doctor indicated a small cabinet next to a sink.

Rising after a quick caress of Eidan's matted hair, Teah collected supplies, ran warm water into a basin, and returned to the bed. She set to work, washing off the smears, drying his skin from his toes up to his scalp, where she stopped and found a comb to tackle his hair and beard. Throughout the process, she kept up a steady commentary describing what she'd done that day, her hopes of things they could do once he recovered, anything that came to mind that didn't refer to the physical trauma he'd undergone. Her hands had shaken when she'd moved the sheet aside to clean his torso, she was so afraid to see his wounds, but they were neatly concealed by sterile wraps. But he was breathing, so she couldn't despair.

His body, now so familiar to her, looked strange in the clinical environment. His muscled legs dusted with hair, his groin, his heavy arms all had been, just that morning, her playground. Now he was inert, unresponsive to her touch as he never had been before. Large dermaseal pieces covered three sections of his broad chest, yellowish stains extending out from under them along his skin and dark red blood seeping under the translucent bandages. She didn't want to think about the damage concealed underneath, how much pain he must have been in. Her brave Eleoni warrior.

By the time she'd finished, the doctor was no longer in the room and Brida was pacing near the now-closed door. Lines of stress bracketed her lips, and she limped slightly. Her clothes were covered with the same mud spatters and smears of dried blood that Teah had just removed from Eidan's body.

"Sit down," Teah urged her as she dragged over a stool. "Are you hurt?"

"A few abrasions. I patched them up myself."

Teah debated suggesting she see the doctor, or even the newly arrived Eleoni medic, but the other woman's tension made her cautious. "At least sit for a moment."

"I shouldn't. I need to report in with the new commander. Acting sheriff now, I suppose." Brida sighed and stared at her prone brother. "Will you stay with him? Until I can return."

"Of course. I'll stay as long you … as long as he needs me."

Brida stared at her for a long minute as if measuring her for some sort of special duty. "Thank you."

The other woman squared her shoulders, stalked to the bed and stroked her brother's hair briefly, then rushed from the room, intent on her mission. Left alone for the first time, Teah took what felt like her first deep breath in hours. She went to Eidan's side again and searched his face for any movement, but he remained still. A glance up at the monitors showed only a confusing jumble of graphs, numbers, and lines of data. He should recover, he *would* recover. The doctor had every confidence, so she would as well.

She threaded her fingers into his soft hair and leaned close to press her lips to his forehead. He smelled like Eidan, musky skin and the slight hint of smoky citrus from the leaf he smoked. Sudden tears welled again, tight in her throat and burning at her eyelids. All she wanted was for him to speak, to move, to smile at her one more time.

Chapter Eight

Eidan pretended to sleep, so he could watch Teah knit. He'd been observing her engage in the peculiar activity for weeks as he recovered and she watched over him, but he was still fascinated by the intricate movements of her fingers and the cast of concentration that transformed her features from beautiful to determined.

He was hopelessly bored, afraid of how weak he'd become, and anxious about Brida's solo investigation into his assassination attempt. He knew she was receiving assistance from the Eleoni reinforcements, but she was also spending a lot of time on her own, forcing interactions with criminals and townsfolk in an effort to shake loose as much evidence as she could before pressing charges. Teah's consistent presence meant his sister could spend her nights prowling Rusk, rousting anyone who caught her eye.

His human sighed and smoothed her hand over the long length of scarf she'd created from a rich, golden colored yarn. She looked up from her work and smiled at him.

"I know you're watching me."

His skills at subterfuge really had deteriorated during his recuperation. At least her finding him out meant he could move and stretch his arms and shoulders. His physical therapy was taking its toll on him, and some days it seemed like his muscles hurt worse than the wounds he'd sustained.

"Very observant of you. Perhaps you should be assisting Brida in her quest." Eidan eased some stiffness out of his joints and winced. Teah tossed her knitting into a basket that had somehow become a permanent fixture in his bedroom and was at his side, her cool hands helping him sit up. She offered a massage, which he accepted with alacrity, and they both worked to remove his shirt. Twinges of pain bolted through him, and he told himself not to worry about it, that he was improving every day even if he longed for the pace to increase so he could resume his duties both at the station and in Teah's bed.

The astringent scent of liniment filled the air, and his human soon began to work at his muscles, stroking along his back, kneading his arms and shoulders. He grunted with slight pain and pure pleasure.

"Do you think she'll make arrests soon?"

"Doubtful. Our position here is still precarious so most residents don't see any return on turning informant. The new Eleoni officers have found it hard going to integrate since their arrival meant we could fire the worst humans, and for some reason, that's being held against us."

Teah laughed at his attempt at humor. "It might also have something to do with the fact that they stride around with those huge guns at the ready. It's a little off-putting."

"Regulation equipment, because of my attack. All humans are considered hostile while martial law is in effect." Brida had declared it as soon as he'd been stabilized in medical, and she showed no inclination to lift it in the future. It made it so much easier for her to pull people in for questioning. Teah kneaded at a particularly tender spot, and he hissed. She immediately pressed a soft kiss to the area, and Eidan smiled. That was certainly something his official physiotherapist never did to ease his pain. "Even you."

She scoffed and lifted his hair up so she could reach his neck. As her fingers stroked he lowered his head to his chest and groaned with pleasure.

"I haven't heard you sound that happy since…" She trailed off, and he knew she was thinking of their last morning together, before he was shot and transformed into a useless shell. He gripped his hands into the sheets and tried not to recall how wet she'd been for him, how her whole body took up the vibrations of her climax. His cock thrummed and stilled. Disappointment filled him.

"I went to the clinic today."

Eidan tensed, his memories of his time confined in that building too new and raw to hold back. "Are you feeling ill?"

"Nothing out of the ordinary. Just headache and stomach upset brought on by stress." Teah moved behind him and angled her body so her breasts were pressing against his back. His glauca prickled all over his body in a cascade of tiny twitches. "I also had a hypothetical question for the doctor."

He mulled on this until Teah nuzzled his ear. He jumped a little. "Are you going to share any of it with me?"

"Of course, since you are the hypothetical in question." There was a teasing tone in her voice, and he tried to twist his head around to catch her eye, but was hampered by the pull of the scar tissue in his chest.

Her hand crept around and pressed against his abdomen, just below the first wound. She kissed his neck and ran her fingernails along the ridges of muscle around his belly button. The fact that her provocative touch didn't stir him filled him with frustrated weariness. The more his body recovered from the attack, he expected his libido to return, but it had not. Teah had been by his side constantly, bathing him, dressing him, touching him in ways that before his injuries would have stimulated his cock to straining attention. But nothing stirred below his waist. She'd never mentioned it or made any direct moves at seduction, and he didn't want to discuss his inability to her.

"I asked her about how long someone should wait to have sex after he or she had been, let's say, injured rather severely."

Trust Teah to express it out so bluntly. So she had been worrying. Eidan hadn't dared ask during any of his appointments, but had instead hoped his cock would spontaneously rise some morning like the sun outside. She stroked the top of his thigh and pressed another kiss to his shoulder.

"And what did she say?"

"It varies from person to person and case to case, of course. Once the injured person is resting well, not in so much pain, and regains some of their normal routine, it's likely. But she did give me some hints on how to trigger those impulses."

Now her hand was resting lightly in his lap, directly over his cock and balls. A little shiver of awareness shook through him. "I do have those impulses, it's just that..."

She cupped him, and he went warm. Her voice tickled into his ear as she wrapped first one leg, then the other around his hips as she pressed tight to his back. "I haven't wanted to pressure you, so I've been keeping my hands to myself."

He laughed, appreciating her effort to make this her problem. To show he wanted the course of this conversation to continue, he placed one of his hands over hers. "So what made you decide to discard that injunction today?"

"You're too sexy to resist."

With a chuckle he again tried to turn his head and meet her gaze, but she kissed the top of his spine instead, just beneath where his hair grew. "How can I be attractive to you? I'm shot full of holes and only last week was I finally able to walk without assistance. All this pain and trouble was my fault. What kind of man falls for a trap like that?"

There was the root of it. His injury, his inattention to his surroundings, his surety that Bokum and his men had been properly cowed, all revealed his weaknesses. And now she had to see him as a patient, not a lover strong enough to protect her.

"Brida fell for it, too, so I don't believe it was that obvious. Your speedy recovery only shows me what a determined man you are." She gently ran her fingers along the length of his cock, and it twitched under her ministrations. "See? You're still there. But I don't want to exhaust you."

He didn't want her to stop. With her soft strokes he was growing harder and even if he couldn't achieve a functional erection, he still craved her touch, could still please her. His hands and tongue worked, after all.

"Lie back," she whispered against his shoulder, her damp breath making his skin pebble. She slid away as he eased himself down on the bed. She returned to his side and kissed him as she pulled at the tapes of his sleep pants. Cool air hit the skin of his groin and legs as she drew the garment away. She'd helped him dress and undress since he'd been hurt, but the glint in her eye was not that of a caregiver intent on healing him.

"Let me take care of everything. Don't even move your arms."

"You forbid me from touching you?" He couldn't keep a touch of asperity from his voice. He wasn't *that* weak.

"Yes. I'm in charge today. By tomorrow you won't let me get away with it."

****

Teah crouched over Eidan and stared at him, hoping to cow him into submission. It had taken a life threatening injury to quiet him, so this might be her only chance to take control of him sexually. She meant to enjoy herself. Not only was she looking forward to a long-awaited orgasm or ten, but she wanted to instill some confidence back in him.

His lavender eyes narrowed and for a second she thought he'd fight her, but then he relaxed his shoulders and settled against the mattress with a sigh. She allowed herself the luxury of looking over his body in an acquisitive manner, rather than as something she had to clean or support. The scars from the pulse bolts that had almost killed him had seared across his chest and left behind shiny pink puckers on his honey skin. But scars meant life, meant he'd survived and healed, so she leaned down and kissed each one, grateful they were there, for the alternative was horrible to contemplate. The scatters of glauca across his shoulders and arms pebbled. He shivered, and she knew he was repressing his urge to touch her hair.

"Aren't they revolting to you?" he whispered, and she shook her head, allowing her lips to trail across his skin.

"I'm glad you have them. They mean you're a fighter. You can show them to your grandchildren someday."

Her stomach plummeted at her offhand remark. Did he think she'd said that as a hint that she wanted to get pregnant? Could a human egg and Eleoni sperm even mesh properly? She assumed not, but that was definitely something she should discuss with her doctor. Bearing children wasn't something she'd spent much time considering. She'd always been too poor on Earth, and now her life on Rusk seemed too precarious to plan that far into the future.

"I don't think it advisable to procreate in this environment. The settlement is too unstable to support a proper school or appropriate recreational facilities I feel children require. I'm sure no one in medical has a pediatric specialization." Eidan blinked, and his lip quirked. "It's an interesting topic, but I'd rather you resume your prior activities at this time. I have a finite amount of strength these days."

"Trying to direct the course?" Teah hoped the relief in her voice didn't show too much. *Babies!* What was going on in her mind?

"No. I leave myself in your capable hands."

That sounded all right by her. Careful not to put any weight on his chest, she licked at one nipple, then the other. They tightened immediately into hard nubs, and he shivered. She wanted to take her time, to caress every centimeter, but he was right, he wouldn't last long, no matter what sort of interaction they could accomplish.

Sliding down his body, she knelt between his spread legs and put her hands beside his hips. Lowering her head, she ran her tongue along his slightly stiff cock, relishing the soft texture of his skin and his musky flavor. By the second circuit of her mouth, he'd swelled and lengthened, and a glow of satisfaction filled her. Taking him in hand she stroked and kissed, giving special attention to the small dent underneath the smooth, wide head. Soon enough he was gasping as his erection filled her mouth and throat, the salty tang of his pre-cum making her salivate.

Sucking on the tip as she squeezed the base of his shaft with her fingers, Eidan groaned loudly and shifted his legs on either side of her.

"Teah, stop ... please," he groaned out, and she released him from her lips with a soft popping sound. His reddish cock was fully engorged and shiny with her saliva and his lubricating fluids. Her pussy was already swollen and wet.

"What do you need, my love?" She didn't care that the endearment had slipped free. She'd been thinking of him that way since she'd seen him lying on that bed, more precious to her when she'd contemplated how close she'd come to losing him. His eyes fluttered open as he stared down at her. She briefly considered drawing out her stimulation until he explicitly begged, but she knew what he wanted.

Releasing his cock, she pulled away her clothes and quickly straddled his hips. Eidan stared up at her as he sucked in deep breaths. He'd pressed his hands against his headboard, and the muscles on his arms stood out in strained swells. He swallowed hard before he spoke. "I've missed you."

Deciding some teasing wouldn't tax him too much, Teah slid his cockhead along the wet crease of her pussy, her whole body tightening with the anticipation of penetration. "I've been here every evening."

"I miss you during the day, when you're working. I missed you doing ... that," he ground out as she allowed the tip of his cock to barely penetrate her, then withdrew him from her body.

"I missed you, too." Teah worked her hips gently, easing more and more of his thick cock into her tight sheath. It had been a while, and she had to go slow as her body gradually relaxed for him. Eidan groaned and closed his eyes when she finally settled against him. She was so thoroughly filled and stretched she thought she could orgasm with only a few rubs of her clit. Fighting to control her breathing and the little flutters of pleasure building in her pussy, she braced her hands on either side of his chest and rocked her hips back and forth a few times, trying not to thrust too hard against him.

He briefly released his hold on the bed. "I want to touch—"

"No, hold still. This is for you, Eidan, as quickly as you can." She meant to encourage him to release as he needed, to not hold back and stress his body in the effort to please her. His eyes opened, and he stared up at her as she continued her movements against him. Her breasts jiggled, and she leaned up and captured them in her hands, manipulating her nipples in the way she knew pleased him. Bracing her knees on the mattress, she rolled her hips, tightening her pussy along his cock with every movement.

"Please let me touch your clit." His arms shook as his breathing grew ragged, and she hoped it was due to an incipient orgasm and not physical exhaustion.

"No. Come in me, Eidan." Her order seemed to trigger something in him, and he threw his head back and let out a guttural groan as his hips flexed under her. She continued rocking as he writhed, gradually slowing as he let his arms fall to the bed and his head lolled to the side. The pungent scent of her fluids and his mingled, and she rejoiced, glad that they'd achieved this milestone together.

Not wanting to put pressure on his chest, she leaned to one side and raised herself to allow his softening cock to slide free of her body. Moisture dripped from her pussy, and her clit throbbed with pent-up tension. Eidan breathed deeply, his eyes closed and for a moment she remembered their first time, how he'd collapsed and she'd been so insulted. He had every right to sleep now.

With a sigh of contentment and unfulfilled arousal, she curled close to his side. With a sleepy murmur he curled one of his arms around her and she rested her thigh on top of his leg. She trailed her fingers down her belly and slid them into the heat of her pussy, drawing their mingled fluids up to her hard clit where she began to circle around but not quite touching, just as she liked. Just as she was relaxing into the burgeoning tension within her, Eidan moved, pulling her leg up over his waist as he rolled to his side. She lost her rhythm for a moment, but returned to it as he clamped his hand on her ass and kissed her forehead.

"May I touch you now?"

"No." She smiled, and he grunted good naturedly at her denial.

"Then you enjoy yourself, little *alati*, and I'll just talk you through." He then began to whisper about all the erotic things he promised to do to her very soon. Her skin tingled with anticipation and the inrushing climax. He mentioned a special toy he'd already ordered, one that would flutter against her clit, vibrate inside her sheath, and probe her anus. How he appreciated how tight she gripped him when she came. "I'll lick your breasts and make them so wet my cock will slide between them like it does in your hot pussy. Then I'll come all over your neck."

As soon as he said come, she did, her whole body shuddering as her fingers worked frantically over her twitching clit. She arched and gusted out a loud moan of dazed relief as waves of pleasure pulsed through her body.

Cradled in his arms, she rested for a moment, enjoying the dizzy whirl of post-climax tingles and shivers. Eidan breathed deeply and stretched his body the way he did when his scar tissue began to itch. She lightly chafed her palm over each wounded area, and he murmured thanks.

"Next time we do this my way."

"I think we should alternate, to be fair." Teah allowed herself the pleasant fantasy that they had a future, that Eidan wouldn't be hurt again, that they would continue to want each other as much as they did now. She knew reality would intrude in this private bubble they'd created while he recovered, but was still in no hurry to venture out into the harshness of Rusk.

****

"I can't believe you're making me do this," whined Dorian as they stood at the front of the line waiting to register for the first official census of Rusk. Teah was nearly hopping with excitement. She couldn't wait for access to the completed list of residents and their dwellings so she could finally begin to construct an efficient delivery route. The call to register had come through official channels, electronic networks, and helpful holographic signs posted on what seemed like nearly every flat surface in town.

She'd collected Dorian from his room at the boarding house and cajoled him the whole way to the new Eleoni administration center housed temporarily in a gutted modular unit sandwiched between a hookah bar and an engine repair shop. There was always a frowning man or woman at the counter, a uniformed officer on loan from the security station conveniently located across the street. The disdain the new lawgivers had for the humans was unmistakable, and understandable since one of their own had nearly died at the hands of some as-yet unidentified group. Teah felt caught in the middle. On the one hand, she was proud to be human and liked many of Rusk's residents, but on the other, the Collective had given her a good job and she'd found unexpected happiness with an Eleoni. So she trod carefully between the two factions, not forcing friendliness with the Eleoni, nor turning her back on people who might have some smidge of information that might lead to Eidan's assailants.

When she reached the counter, she smiled at the Eleoni on duty. They didn't wear nametags or introduce themselves, so she had no idea of the woman's name. Dorian hovered at her shoulder.

"Hello, I'm here to register. My name is—"

"I'm aware." The woman drawled as she looked up and down Teah's uniform. Teah's shoulders went back and she tugged at her tunic, suddenly worried she'd buttoned up wrong that morning. No, Eidan would have told her, teased her about disregarding regulations as he unbuttoned her and slid his hands underneath to…

"Sheriff Cozad has already dealt with you." The Eleoni officer said, one corner of her full lip curling up as she glanced at a monitor in front of her.

"But I thought I had to report in person."

"You're done. Next?" The woman dismissed her without even a glance, and Teah automatically stepped to the side for Dorian to present himself.

"Don't I have to provide my personal scan?" Teah wasn't sure why she was pursuing this other than her inherent need to follow procedure. The Eleoni was making it abundantly clear she didn't want to interact with Teah any longer. The officer turned bright turquoise eyes on Teah and spoke slowly, as if to a fussy child.

"The Sheriff has input all your data. Highly irregular, but I suppose he can do as he likes with his … human entertainment."

Teah's mouth fell open, then closed with a snap. Dorian stared wide-eyed between the two of them and clutched his personal data chip close to his chest. She hadn't explicitly told anyone she and Eidan were involved personally, but she was sure Bokum's minions certainly knew what was happening between them since she spent every night with the sheriff. For some reason she'd been reluctant to tell her friend, and now he'd found out from a disdainful third party.

"Please excuse me for bothering you," Teah ground out and stalked from the building, a simmering anger burning in her belly. She waited for Dorian and wondered who offended her more, Eidan for his high-handedness, the Eleoni officer for her rudeness, or just people in general for being so judgmental. On top of that, she'd have to deal with whatever reaction her friend might have.

Dorian popped out of the door before she had time to decide what to say. He stared at her and shook his head.

"What the collapsing worm hole are you doing, Teah?"

She started to answer, then thought better of it since Dorian was clearly in a state. Instead, she turned and walked towards the post office, the sudden urge to get behind her counter and organize packing materials paramount on her mind. Dorian's arm snaked out, and he grabbed her elbow.

"Are you—" Dorian paused and glanced around, then towed her to the entrance of a narrow alley that smelled of rotten eggs. "Please tell me you aren't friends with him."

Embarrassment made her cheeks flare hot and she skittered her gaze from his, unable to bear the concern in his stare. He had no idea where she'd been spending her evenings since he worked the night shift. "There's nothing wrong with him. He's a nice person, his sister is too."

Dorian shook his head quickly. "You just feel sorry for him because he was hurt, right? Just like when you rescued your aircuttle. General kindness for a creature in need. He's an alien, not at all like us, Teah. You can't trust them."

Teah swallowed, distressed that Eidan had been compared to an animal by her good friend. "He's the sheriff. He's here to help—"

"Are you joking? He and his kind are here to tax us and rule us. You saw how they treated you back there. Have you seen the list of regulations business owners have to follow now? After registering their business for a hefty fee, of course."

Dorian's angry tone surprised her. She hadn't paid much attention to the new rules since her business was public service and she'd been mightily distracted with Eidan lately. She'd heard mutters of discontent from people waiting in line at the post office, but she'd tuned it out.

Her friend frowned as he studied her face. "Wait a minute, that Eleoni described you as a, what was it, the sheriff's 'human entertainment'. What does that even mean? Are you some sort of game to him, or…"

As he trailed off, his eyes widened, and his mouth fell open. "No, Teah, don't tell me you and he are—"

"Then don't ask." Teah snapped as she shook off his hold, her humiliation now complete. She never discussed her sex life with Dorian. Doing so would have been uncomfortable to them both.

"That's disgusting." Dorian breathed out as he took a step away, right into a puddle covered by an oily sheen. Did he think she was somehow infected by Eleoni particles transferred by skin-to-skin contact?

Anger bloomed in her chest with the heat of the sun. Enough of this shaming. "Dorian, I can't believe you would hold such prejudices."

"It's not prejudice. It's a different *species*, Teah. It's unnatural. Don't you realize what you've done?"

All she'd done was fall in love. *Love*. The realization hit her like a dropped coral ball, and she blinked, suddenly unaware of anything else around. What would happen now? She'd jumped into bed with a powerful man who she didn't know very well, who happened to belong to a culture she was nearly entirely ignorant about. And she'd lost her heart to him. She wouldn't have any idea of the cues he might be giving as to how he felt about her, or what he wanted from their relationship. Stars, on Eleon, having sex with someone might not mean much more than shaking hands did to humans.

Their relationship meant more to her, much more, and now she was adding a whole plethora of emotions and needs on her part with no hint of reciprocity from him. She'd been foolish, believing the intimacy of the care she'd given him was somehow binding them together when he might take it as a simple matter of charity.

"What I've done is my business, Dorian. You're my friend. You're not supposed to judge me."

"I'm not judging you. Well, maybe I am a little because Eleoni are so, ah, unfriendly to us. But you need to consider how other people are going to react to this. You're a human, and you need to be on the side of humans."

"What sides? Aren't we all here to work together?" Even as she said it, she knew it sounded naïve and unrealistic. Dorian was here to make money, she was here to start her career, Eidan was here to do his duty. A fever to confront him came over her in a hot, flustered wave. "Listen, I have to go."

"Don't go to him. You'll regret it. People won't forgive you for this." Dorian's pleadings made her heart ache. He genuinely had her best interests at heart, but she was going to Eidan, whose best interests remained a mystery. He'd never expressed deep affection or devotion, but merely talked with her about any topic and enjoyed sexual gymnastics with her. Perhaps his preemptive registration of her was a sign of regard rather than him taking control.

Without saying another word to Dorian, Teah fled, heading towards the post office since she had to put in a four hour shift at the counter, then make a delivery to the science station. Perhaps the time spent apart from Eidan would calm her and she wouldn't rush to him demanding he love her in return.

****

Eidan rubbed at the glauca on his ribs and winced as they stung. When Teah touched them, waves of pleasure tickled his skin, but now the brush of his shirt was a torment. His head ached again. This discomfort was on top of the throb of each of the three puncture wounds on his chest, repaired courtesy of nanoparticles, but still significantly altered from his original structure.

"Do you need a pain reliever?" Brida spoke up from her seat in the living area. She was busy coordinating all the clandestine monitoring equipment she and the other security staff had set up on the sly, keeping the gathered information to the Eleoni officers only. No humans, security or civilian, had any idea the extent they were now being observed.

"No." Eidan tried to talk himself out of feeling discontented. It didn't work. A small wave of nausea rolled in his gut. "I think I'm becoming ill."

At that admission, his sister rose and walked to his side, peering in his face like she could detect microorganisms with her bare eyes. "What's wrong? How do you feel?"

Her worry disabled his usual impulse to keep his distress to himself. He'd been severely injured and perhaps was still too weak to recover from a simple infection. "I have a headache and my glauca burn. Sometimes I feel sick in the pit of my stomach."

Brida's eyebrows shot up, and she leaned closer. "When does your stomach feel upset? In the morning, during the day, or in the evening?"

"Only during the day. What does that matter?"

His sister pursed her lips and nodded once like she'd solved a great conundrum. "How long have you had these symptoms?"

Eidan paused to consider. Being shot and his long recovery had somewhat scrambled his memory. "Since we arrived here. Perhaps I'm allergic to something on this planet." It was certainly possible considering all the unknown contaminants which certainly lurked in the wet soil and humid air of Rusk.

"But in the evening, when Teah is here, you feel better?"

Of course he did. His human's presence was a lovely balm on these interminable days he had to spend before resuming his full duties. A man could only get so much satisfaction from filing reports and collating information feeds. At his nod of agreement, his sister grinned hugely.

"I know exactly what's wrong with you."

"Then reveal it. I want to gain treatment immediately so this ailment won't delay my return to the station."

"There's nothing medical can do for you. I take that back, I suppose they could formulate something to help you, but it's nothing a human doctor has any experience with. You'd have to see a specialist on Eleon if you want to be cured."

His gut, previously doing a slow roll, now churned with tension. "What *is* it, Brida?"

She giggled. His sister never giggled. "You've melded! All the signs are there. I remember the first few weeks with Wil, my skin was on fire when he wasn't there to soothe me and I felt like my brain had swollen to twice its size whenever he was gone."

Eidan shook his head once, denying her assertion since it was completely ridiculous. "Melded with who?"

"Teah, you dunce! Who else?"

"But she's human." It was impossible. Melds occurred between Eleoni only. It was one of the defining traits of their race, just as Kotze possessed hyperflexible fingers and Ra'uf shed their teeth every five years. No other sentient species modified its own body chemistry to increase compatibility between a mated pair.

"You've melded to her. All the symptoms fit, and the time you've spent together has only accelerated the process, I'd guess. The only question is, has she melded to you?"

Eidan stood up and paced the length of the living room. It was impossible. "No."

Brida went on as if she hadn't heard him. "It's no wonder we were so easily ambushed. I was recovering from my dying meld and you were fresh into yours. We didn't quite add up to a complete officer at that point." His sister burbled out a laugh. "You'll see. She'll arrive and your mood will improve, your head will stop hurting, and as soon as she touches your glauca it'll be like the most soothing comfort. Here I thought you two were simply vigorous lovers!"

Eidan gave her a snarl in response, so overwhelmed by the idea he wasn't sure what to say. The door alarm sounded, and he accessed the monitor, grateful for the interruption. Brida let out a giggle and rushed to the door, flinging it open and greeting Teah with a quick hug. She pulled his human in and dragged her forward, presenting her with a flourish.

"Look, Eidan! It's Teah. Isn't that wonderful? Do you feel better now?" Brida's cheerful questions irritated Eidan beyond measure, and he pushed aside the hand she tried to place on his forehead as if searching for a fever. Teah blinked at his sister's effusive greeting and then stared at Eidan with a slight frown.

"You aren't feeling well? What's wrong?" She reached out for his hands, and at her touch, all the agitated nerve endings in his body cooled and his heart pounded. It couldn't be a meld—he didn't want one. Even if there was some transformation on his part, for he had to acknowledge that something had changed within him, it was still impossible. She couldn't change along with him as he needed her to. If he melded, that is. He'd be linked to her, trailing after her like a lovesick fool, and she would feel nothing.

"I'm fine." He straightened his shoulders and told himself he still had a headache, that his skin still itched, denying Brida's ridiculous claim. Those symptoms were probably some side effect of his injuries.

"I came to tell you I tried to register today, and to check on you of course." Teah stepped closer, a soft light in her eye as she looked up at him, clearly wishing to be greeted with a kiss. He didn't bend down to capture her mouth as he'd done every evening for the past few weeks, and something in his neck throbbed. She blinked once.

"I tried to register, but the officer said you'd already done it."

"I did." He swallowed past some sort of obstruction in his throat. Brida took a step back and lowered her brows.

"I'll just be going to check on the feeds at the station." His sister gave him a searing glare, then wrapped her slicker around before plunging out into the wet darkness.

Teah leaned his way and circled an arm around his waist as she laid her head against his shoulder. "Are you really all right? I can call the clinic if you like."

"I don't need a doctor." Eidan extricated himself from her soft embrace and stalked toward the kitchen, telling himself to get a drink of water to clear his dry mouth. He fumbled with the glass and spigot until Teah appeared at his side to quickly take over and offer him a drink.

"I can fill a glass for myself. I'm not incapacitated any longer." Eidan knew his tone was too sharp, knew it wasn't fair to chastise her in any way since she was merely helping as she had all along, but he was too agitated to stop himself.

"I never said you were incapacitated."

"But I was and you saw it." He gulped down a drink. The cool liquid didn't refresh him as it should have. His gut burned.

She nodded slowly. "I did, and you're so much better now—"

"Exactly. I'm better. I don't want you to feel like you need to check on me every evening any longer. I'm managing very well on my own."

Teah's soft lips fell open, and her eyes widened. "Oh. Are you saying…"

"I'm saying I'm fine and thank you for all your help. You were very kind." Eidan sucked in a pained breath, his heart galloping as his skin went cold. There was a roaring in his ears, and he suddenly wished he could sit down.

"You want me to leave?" Her question came out in an agonized whisper as tears glittered along her eyelashes.

"Yes, that's for the best. I'm very tired, and tomorrow I plan on being at the station for a half day."

"So you need your rest." Teah backed away and tightened her trembling lips. "I understand. Broose will be glad to have me for the evening. He's been missing me, I think. Let me know if you … if you need anything."

"Good night." That damned farewell left his lips and he wanted to snatch it back, gather in all the dismissive things he'd thrown at her. What had he just done?

With a quiet sniff, she turned and trotted to the door. She flung it open and disappeared into the night, fading into the shadows but not so quickly that he didn't hear her sob. Pain twisted his temples, and he staggered. It was for the best, to gain some distance from each other. He hadn't melded with her, he'd just fallen into an infatuation intensified by his injury and the sweetness she'd shown him afterwards. The only thing different about his body was the scars on his chest.

Stumbling to the sofa, he toppled forward and lay down, not quite aware of his surroundings as the room spun around him.

****

What a fool she was, what an utter, abject fool. Teah shuffled along a walkway, the tears in her eyes nearly blinding her to how close to the edge she'd veered. Eidan didn't love her. He didn't even want her around now that he was better. Cold realization stabbed deep in her heart, and she moaned at the pain. She'd cared for him, opened her body and soul to him, and he'd taken what he'd needed as his due, then dismissed her because he wanted to sleep. She should have paid attention to the first time and realized he'd simply repeat the pattern.

Swallowing back the sobs that ached in her throat, she looked around, blinking away the tears. She'd only managed to cross the street from his house and it felt like she'd been walking for miles. Succumbing to weakness, she glanced back at his front door, illuminated by a steady, bright light. No, he wasn't there, ready to call her back or crossing the muddy expanse to sweep her up and carry her back for apologies and a tender reconciliation. Damn him.

Too late she remembered Bokum's men and the likelihood they were lurking about. Urging her clumsy feet forward, she headed for the bright lights and milling crowds of the entertainment section. She'd be distracted from her misery there and might even stop by the Last Chance and sit in on a game of Dorian's. Shaking her head, she knew she was fooling herself. She was going to scuttle back to her little home and cry for hours. She just had to get there and not break down before she shut her door on the world.

By the time she reached the nearest intersection, she thought she was home free and breathed out a sigh of relief. How could he just reject her like that? He'd been so cold, his features so tight and unlike his usual—

"Not so fast, little parcel." A deep, unfamiliar voice startled her even as a strong hand grabbed her elbow. She spun on her heels as her captor dragged her toward a narrow, dark alley. A heavy hand slammed over her mouth before she could let out a startled squeal. Shock froze her still for a moment, but then fear took over and she struggled against the big man that held her.

"Stop it, or I'll have to knock you out. Fist or drug, whatever strikes me. Or you." A low chuckle followed the threat, and she went still in his restricting grip. Without warning she was lifted off her feet and carried deeper into the darkness as rain pattered around them. She scrabbled at any parts of his body she could reach, but her struggles didn't even make him alter his stride.

His grip on her was tight enough to make her lose her breath and she was seeing blinking lights in her peripheral vision by the time he stopped and propped her on her numb feet. Before she could react, he bound her wrists together with something soft. His path had been so circuitous she'd lost all sense of direction, and her disorientation persisted when her kidnapper nudged her into a seated position on a hard surface, then strapped her down. She opened her mouth to speak or scream, and he leaned forward to face her, a stray beam of light illuminating his high cheekbones and arched nose. Dark eyes with thick lashes bored into hers.

"No noise, my little parcel. You're doing so well." He dipped his gaze lower. "I don't want to have to gag that pretty mouth."

Teah waited for some crude reference, but it never came. He simply arched up a swooping brow and waited for her acquiescence. She jerked out a quick nod, too frightened and confused to put up much resistance. She glanced around and managed to make out that he'd placed her in the jump seat of a small, sleek cart parked in a long, low enclosed space. He sat down next to her, made a few adjustments to his dark grey clothing and the vehicle's controls, and then they were moving past looming pallets of wrapped material. A warehouse, probably one at the south end of Rusk judging by how quickly he'd carried her there.

They sped along in silence for a few moments, whipping from one warehouse into another. Then he drove them through an open door that barely accommodated the sides of the cart and they were in a small shed barely containing a huge, battered ore wagon. Without slowing, the man drove the mini cart up the loading ramp and into the bed of the mega hauler.

He swung out of his seat as the cart coasted to a stop, and Teah craned her neck to watch him as he strode across the decking and activated the ramp. With a screech, it rose, clanging, closed with a bang, and they were again in darkness. Lights clicked on around the perimeter, and she took in the surroundings. It wasn't an ore hauler any more. The big open space designed to be filled with rubble and debris was clean, with a few monitors attached to the walls. A table folded down from a large metal bulkhead, with two chairs pulled up next to it. Cozy for an impromptu jail.

The man approached her, and she got her first good look at him. He was striking with black wavy hair and a hawk-like nose but even more remarkably he was clean. His dark clothes were neatly tailored and crisp, and there was hardly a speck of mud on him. Obviously a new arrival on planet. He took a small device from his pocket and waved it over her body, unfastening her from the seat and helping her step out from the cart so he could check her back and bottom. He then rummaged through her bag with quick efficiency, only pausing over her knitting bag as he withdrew her needles and tossed them into a corner.

He drew back and read the results with a shrug. "I anticipated he had you chipped already which meant I had to get you in here and scrambled very quickly, but you're clean."

Teah swallowed, ready to venture a question now. "Who would chip me?"

"Why, your sheriff paramour, of course."

"He's not my paramour." Teah was surprised at the anger in her voice. She should be frightened to immobility by being kidnapped, but instead Eidan's rejection was uppermost in her mind. Her skin went cold, and she shivered.

"According to my employers, the man is your lover and knowing Eleoni as I do, I'm more than a little surprised he hasn't secured his mate more tightly. Very possessive of their things, as I have good cause to know." He flexed his fingers like he was grasping something small.

"Then that just goes to show I'm not his … his mate or anything else." Teah couldn't stop the quaver in her voice, the new, searing grief at Eidan's rejection tightening in her chest like her heart was going to explode. Tears formed at the corners of her eyes, and to her utter humiliation, they began to drip down her cheeks. Since her hands were restrained, she couldn't wipe them away. Just what she wanted to do, cry in front of this dapper criminal.

He raised one eyebrow and matter-of-factly pulled a square of soft cloth from a pocket and daubed away her tears. He probably made lots of people cry with his kidnapping and threats.

"You were leaving his home in the evening, and my intelligence indicates you've spent the night there on numerous occasions, so pardon my assumptions."

"Your intelligence," Teah scoffed, not caring if he was going to retaliate in a physically abusive manner. A beating on her body would match the pain in her heart. This was turning into the worst night of her life.

He nodded and shrugged. "My information in this case is dependent of the observations of my employer's henchmen. Since he no longer maintains much confidence in them, evidenced by my arrival on this mudball of a planet, I am inclined to doubt them as well."

"Then let me go. I mean nothing to Eidan Cozad. He's not going to care that you have me." As soon as the words left her mouth an unstoppable sob burst out of her and she heaved out a cry.

"My contract says to hold you until further notice, and hold you I shall." He again wiped her face, and she sniffled, whispering thanks and wondering why she was being polite to a hired gun.

"Now, since I have no idea how long we might be in each other's company, how about we get comfortable?" He reached for her arms, and she shrank back, her sadness disappearing as she flinched. What was he going to do to her? As soon as she moved, he held up his hands in an appeasing gesture.

"Please, I don't mean to harm you."

"Pardon me if I don't believe you. You have kidnapped me and threatened to hit and drug me, after all."

He took a step to one side and regarded her with narrowed eyes. "True on the first count, and the second was an either/or proposition that was merely a threat to keep you quiet until I could get you to this secure location. Scream all you like now." He waved at the thick sides of the hauler.

Right. "So you expect me to believe you aren't going to hurt me?"

"A peculiar life has taught me to have no expectations when it comes to another's behavior. I *hope* you'll believe me when I assure you no harm will come to you if you don't cause a fuss."

Why shouldn't she cause a fuss? Sighing back that unhelpful retort, Teah tried to regain some composure. Against all evidence to the contrary, her captor wasn't frightening her in any way, other than the obvious held-against-her-will issue. To assess his sincerity, she held out her bound hands and he immediately moved to unfasten them.

He placed a palm against his chest and gave a small bow. "Our precipitous meeting prevented a proper introduction. I am Venture, solver of sticky situations."

"I'm no sticky situation."

"My employer believes you are the solution to his sticky situation. With you as a bargaining chip, he hopes to achieve some leverage with the sheriff. Come to an understanding, a meeting of the minds, what have you." Venture made a come along gesture with one long-fingered hand.

"Bokum's doomed to disappointment then." Teah frowned but took the seat the man offered her. She was sore and shaky and wasn't quite sure how she should be feeling at the moment. Venture sat opposite her, glanced at some of his glowing monitors, then turned his attention back to her.

"So you keep asserting. I take it your assignations with Sheriff Cozad were less than meaningful."

"Of course not," Teah said, insulted at the implication. "At least, not on my part."

Venture made an ah-ha sound, and leaned forward as if very interested. She decided at that moment, what was the harm in unburdening herself. It might make Venture slightly sympathetic to her cause.

"So Cozad is one of those superficial types. Interesting. I wouldn't have guessed that from his bio."

"I'm sure he's very committed to his duties and family. Just not to me." Sadness weighted her chest, and she sighed.

"Short-sighted on his part. You seem a lovely young woman. But if there's no meld, there's no meld. Don't take it personally."

Teah shook her head briefly. "What meld?"

Venture settled back in the posture of a man who enjoyed expressing his knowledge to the less informed. "It's an Eleoni custom. Well, to be accurate, it's a physiological process and not something under their conscious control, although there are medical therapies available.

"Eleoni can form attachments, just as we humans can, with all the attendant emotional and hormonal outbursts, but there is sometimes an even stronger reaction between lovers, one where the body produces chemicals that mirror those found in the other party or parties. Their cells are altered in such a way that emotional health and physical comfort are dependent on proximity to the beloved."

It was such a strange idea Teah couldn't respond for a moment. "Well, it apparently doesn't work across species. How do you know so much about it?"

"My business dealings require me to be a student of all cultures. The Eleoni are powerful force in this quadrant, so I've applied myself to their study, to the amusement and pleasure of several select Eleoni women."

"You mean they have money and you need to know how to scam them to get it."

Venture laughed charmingly and nodded. "That cuts to the quick of it. In any case, you have my sympathies if your feelings toward the man were unrequited, but there are other prospects on the horizon."

He smoothed his hand down his chest, and Teah almost laughed. It wouldn't do to become too chummy with a man she couldn't trust any farther than her misplaced knitting needles.

"So, how does this work? Am I going to be ransomed or tortured in front of him?" Teah wanted to sound brave and blasé, but she knew she couldn't pull it off. Another pang of grief threaded through her veins. "He wouldn't pay a pip to save me."

"I don't think my employer has an especially solid grasp on the possible outcomes of his rather unstable plan. I demanded the majority of my payment up front since I didn't have a good feeling about how things will work out for Bokum."

"Good for you to cover your end," Teah said with more than a little anger. She'd probably end up dead in Bokum's illogical pursuit of some sort of victory over Eidan.

"Fret not. There's nothing in it for me to see you hurt and in fact, Collective sanctions are ever so much harsher for homicide than they are for simple kidnapping. I have to weigh risk versus reward. If turning you over to Bokum looks as if it would result in your demise, I won't do it, since I'd be an accessory."

"That's a very fine distinction to make."

"And I make them so well." Venture preened. "Now, since we will be whiling away a good amount of time, what would you like? Some tea or something stronger?"

Chapter Nine

Eidan wanted to retch into the trash receptacle by his feet, but he controlled his stomach with a mighty effort. Ever since Teah had left the night before, ever since he'd pushed her away, rather, he'd been struck with a powerful malaise strong enough to make him consider not even getting out of bed that morning. It was too important to put on an appearance at the safety station that morning, to prove to the human population he was recovered and in control once again, so he'd stumbled through a shower, dressed in a uniform in the hopes the stiff seams and thick belt would help hold him up, and reported in.

Brida was keeping a close eye on him as he concluded the staff meeting with his new officers. It was a relief to see so many well-trained and motivated Eleoni. As soon as he'd dismissed them to patrol, he sank into a seat and gripped his throbbing head. His sister rushed to his side.

"I knew this was too much for you. Is your chest hurting?"

"No, it's not that. I'm just coming down with something."

"Oh, that. You know what the problem is there. Couldn't Teah stay the night? I'm telling you, you need to be around her at this point or you're going to feel awful constantly. Once your system settles into it, you'll manage when you're apart."

"No. She didn't stay. I told her to go."

Brida drew back with a hiss of indrawn breath. "You're such an idiot. You *rejected* her? No wonder you feel like excrement." She thumped his back. "Get on over to the postal office and apologize."

Even as he shook his head he was standing, the idea of seeing Teah, begging forgiveness, energized him. Why was he fighting this? He wanted to be with her, longed to see her, her touch was a joy to his body and soul. There was no need to be fixated on whether or not he'd melded with her or if she harbored strong enough feelings for him. What mattered was being with her again. He'd never even discussed his feelings with her and some openness was long overdue.

"Go on, I'll manage the office while you make amends. Do a good job, brother."

He left his sister with a wave and exited the building, barely paying attention to where he placed his feet or who he passed as he made his way to the postal office. He reached the door, his heart lifting at the thought of her being just inside, probably very angry with him, but there for him to woo regardless. The door did not open. He tried again and peered into the dim interior. No lights were on. He then stepped back and surveyed the building. Mud spattered halfway up the sides of the structure, a clear indicator Teah hadn't yet descended from her home atop the building. She never would have been able to walk past such a mess. She never would have abandoned her post.

He accessed his PD and called her. No reply, no signal that his call had been delivered.

Eidan bounded up the stairs and activated her home door monitor again and again. At the third interval with no answer, an accelerating sense of wrongness invaded his system and he decided to break a rule and input her security code. The door swung open at his prompt and a bright orange Broose immediately rushed out, whirling around his head and hissing.

"Where is she?" he asked the cephalopod, not expecting an answer as he stepped inside the small apartment. It was perfectly neat and tidy, and Teah was nowhere to be found. The bag she'd had with her the previous evening was also missing. Was it possible she hadn't even made it home last night?

He made another call, which went unanswered. His heart was racing, and he told himself to calm down and logically approach the problem. He called Brida, and she answered immediately. He filled her in on the situation before she could begin to tease him about groveling to Teah and she swung into action. Before he even had Teah's door closed, confining a complaining Broose, his sister was pulling up all available views of his human's exit from his home the evening before. He heard Brida's indrawn breath and knew something terrible had happened.

"Describe." He forced himself to calm as he descended the stairs and jogged back to the station, every step jarring the newly-healed wounds on his chest.

"Someone snatched her across the street from our place. The visual feed angle misses the grabber, but you can clearly see a dark arm reach out and pull her under a roof edge, out of range."

Damn Bokum. Damn him to the lowest pits of magma on Rihold.

"Eidan, do not act in haste. Return so we can formulate a plan," his sister pleaded.

"I'm going to decapitate him."

"Not yet. We need to ensure Teah's safety before you have your revenge."

Eidan felt his lips pull back as he bared his teeth in a primitive snarl. He wanted to tear every tottering building in this dilapidated town apart until he found her. If she'd come to harm, if she'd been even so much as bruised, he'd see the whole lot of humans bound for interment, with any who'd touched her strung up by the short hairs.

"What's her tracking signal?"

His stomach clenched into an icy ball. Why hadn't he seduced her into being chipped? Was he so small-minded to not even consider it because she was human? "She doesn't have one."

Brida's shocked intake of breath compounded the regret and rage he was pouring on himself.

"She would have said no." Eidan ground out the words, desperate for Brida to employ some sort of fantastic investigatory magic and simply tell him what direction to go. He'd never asked about chipping Teah, afraid she'd argue, and now she was gone.

"Oh, Eidan. I'm so sorry." His sister made a sympathetic little noise then briskly ordered him to return to the station. Despite all his instincts clamoring for him to find his human, save her from harm, bring her back to his life where she belonged, he instead charged down Teah's narrow stairs and ran back to the station, ignoring the pain in his chest as best he could.

****

"This is interesting." Venture looked up from his third attempt to cast on some fingerling yarn and stared at one of the monitors. Teah rose slightly from her seat next to him to get a better look at what was happening in Rusk, at least what was happening within range of the Eleoni visual monitors the criminal had managed to tap into. She'd been shocked to discover how much of the settlement was under observation.

She and her captor had whiled away most of the morning with an impromptu knitting lesson after she'd spent a fitful night sleeping on a small pallet he'd put together for her. It had been a fairly amicable confinement, but what was happening in the main intersection of Rusk was anything but.

A platoon of heavily armored Eleoni strode into view, weapons held ready as they took up position in front of all the main businesses. Humans scattered and clustered in watchful clumps as the law enforcers stared back. An Eleoni in armor strode to the center of the intersection and stood directly in front of the Last Chance Gambling Hall. Teah sucked in a breath. It was Eidan. She could tell from his posture and the slight hitch in his walk. Her heart fluttered.

"So that's your man there." Venture dropped his knitting and activated something under the monitor. Audio hissed to life.

"Bokum, I hereby demand you present yourself for arrest pursuant to the warrant just issued." Eidan's voice rang out, and she shivered. Damn the man for arousing her with just his voice when she hated him.

"Your man is bold," Venture said with a smile in his voice.

"He's not my man."

There was a bustle of people emerging from the Last Chance. Teah thought she recognized one who'd said terrible things to her. They all lined up at the instruction of the officers waiting outside and were quickly divested of any concealed weapons.

"Does he think you're in there?"

"I don't care what he thinks."

Venture slid his gaze from the scene playing out several hundred meters away from their current location. "It's a chancy move. Bokum could drag you out there by your neck. If you were there."

"If he did that, Eidan would tear his throat out with his teeth." The certainty of it flooded Teah with courage. Even if Eidan didn't love her, he'd still protect her as he would anyone else under his care.

"Passionate fellow." Venture's mild tone didn't dispel the slight shading of speculation in his voice. Both she and Venture started when an explosion cracked out from the monitor. Smoke billowed from the entrance to the Last Chance and several of the Eleoni rushed in, heedless of the debris. Eidan stalked behind them and disappeared from view. Almost immediately chairs and tables came flying out of the windows to shatter and sink into the muddy street, followed by several gaming machines that blinked wildly then began to smoke. Eidan must be wreaking havoc inside.

Teah took a breath and told her rebellious body to cool down. "What are you going to do with me?"

Venture drew back from the destructive scene playing on the monitor like a piece of debris might fly out and injure his face. "I'm thinking cutting my losses is the most propitious choice."

Teah stared at him. "Are you going to kill me?"

"And have that maniac chase me across the Schetel star field?" The man shook his head steadily as he rose from his seat. "I'm going to consider my retainer payment in full for this job."

A squawk of noise from the monitor brought their attention back to the action. A few human men tumbled from the Last Chance, herded by Eleoni with weapons trained on them. Then Eidan emerged, one hand grasping the collar of a hunched figure Teah recognized as Bokum. The human man flailed his arms and dragged on his knees as Eidan pulled him to the center of the intersection in sight of all the residents who'd gathered around. The sheriff's voice thundered out loud enough to make Teah jump. Her skin prickled hot and cold, and she chastised herself for the involuntary clench of her pussy.

"Anyone with information regarding the whereabouts of the planetary postal officer Teah Riuda is to report to the security station immediately to offer a statement. Rewards will be granted to any person whose information leads to her recovery."

"Reward sounds like a nice option," her captor said with a pleased curl in his low voice.

Teah couldn't take her eyes away from Eidan as he marched out of the frame, Bokum bouncing along in his wake. "You expect to get a reward for returning me when you were the one who kidnapped me in the first place?"

"To be fair, your Eleoni has the true culprit in custody. I was merely a subcontractor."

She couldn't hold back her exasperated sigh. This Venture fellow was quite a trial. "How do you propose to make this exchange?"

"You let me worry about that. This sort of interaction is my forte."

"You bet I'm going to let you worry about that."

****

The doctor finally left the station, his mouth clamped in a grim crease as Brida followed him to the door, her face set in equally displeased lines. All the men and women arrested had insisted they be examined by trained medical personnel, some claiming injuries, others bellowing about the possibility of being tortured while in custody. It was all quite tedious and did nothing to alleviate Eidan's fever to find Teah. So far, none of the interviews had resulted in any tangible leads and he was ready to slam some furniture around.

Brida returned to his desk and took her usual place at his side, huffing loudly. "That man is deliberately obstructive. And arrogant."

"The doctor? He seemed to perform his duties to the letter." Eidan answered absently, scanning the sat scans of the settlement, looking for any heat signatures in isolated structures that could be Teah under confinement. So far, none had been her. He'd already rushed out on three raids that had resulted in an encounter with one of the dogs Teah had described to him, and the other two were humans merely sleeping off drug binges. Where could she be?

"I don't believe we will gain any information from these humans. It's time to search building to building." It was his last chance to find her, barring the idea that she'd somehow been secreted to a ship and wasn't on planet any longer, or had been transported out to some location in the forest.

"It'll take a while," Brida said with a cautioning tone. He knew she was trying to introduce the idea that he needed to begin to consider the more awful alternatives to finding Teah alive and well and hidden in a closet or storage room.

He paced to a weapons locker and opened it, not interested in more conversation, more delays. His hand grasped a phase rifle without much conscious consideration, and he hefted into his arms, the familiar weight a comfort.

"Planning on leveling half a block?" Brida asked as she grabbed her own rifle.

"It's a start." His stomach burned in counterpoint to the fire wreathing his temples. He'd forged a meld with a human woman, unbelievable as that was, and now she was taken from him. It was an excruciating situation, and he had to find relief in some way. Taking the hard line with some petty criminals was going to have to serve.

The sound of the station door opening interrupted his dire thoughts. He turned, ready to remonstrate but was shocked to silence when he saw Teah standing there, a slim and tall human man standing behind her. Her deep brown eyes were wide, and her normally tidy hair hung in wispy strands from her head. She was the most beautiful woman he'd ever seen.

He whispered her name, and she frowned. She tightened her soft lips and resolutely turned her face toward Brida. "I heard there was a reward for my return. Is that true?"

His sister nodded. "That's correct, but since you're here of your own volition—"

"Not really. This man—" Teah gestured at the human behind her. The man in dark clothing smoothed the front of his immaculate coat and put on a bland smile. "Has returned me, so to speak, so he should get the reward."

Eidan forced himself to stop staring at Teah and instead assessed the stranger. Not filthy enough to be a native and far too relaxed in the presence of law enforcement and weapons to be anything other than a criminal. And he was standing quite close to Teah. That was unacceptable.

"Move back." Eidan gestured at a far corner of the station reception room and the human man's eyes narrowed briefly, but his face quickly smoothed into a semblance of pleasantness. He raised his hands in an appeasing gesture and retreated a step. Teah lowered her brows and followed him, placing herself between them.

"Brida, Deputy Cozad, is there a reward or isn't there?"

"There isn't one for him," Eidan ground out, sensing something highly irregular between Teah and the man.

"Then I shall excuse myself promptly." The stranger backed away, aiming unerringly toward the door without taking his eyes from Eidan. "It's been lovely. A pleasure to visit a new planet with such potential for profit. With Eleoni supervision and benevolent guidance, of course."

Teah half turned toward the man and frowned at him. "Don't you want your money, Venture?"

"Ah, not especially," he replied. "Risk versus reward, my dear."

"She's not your dear." Eidan knew he was growling but didn't particularly care to shade his voice in a more civilized tone. The illness which had been plaguing him for hours eased, along with some of the shame and fear he'd been carrying. Teah was there.

"I'm not *your* dear, either," Teah whispered as she slanted a hot look his way, then turned her attention to his sister. "I'm just reporting in that I'm fine, no need to send out search parties and make a ruckus in town. People out there look a little rattled."

"You stay right there." Eidan reached out for her arm, the only properly sanctioned place he could touch her now that they were estranged. Well, he'd have them un-estranged once he got a moment alone with her. Teah twisted away and again shook her head at him. His cock hardened, and he anticipated a long session of reminding her of how exquisite it was for both of them when she complied with his wishes.

"He's gone," Brida announced, and Teah looked around.

The stranger had disappeared out the front door while Eidan had been distracted. Damn it to the planet's core, her likely kidnapper had slipped away. He activated his desk communicator and called up the port authority. "Continue to hold all ships until further notice."

An irritated voice agreed then mumbled about the way martial law was playing havoc with his schedules. Eidan cut him off and reached out again for Teah, capturing her elbow and holding tight. She already had a hand on the door and hadn't even said a proper hello to him.

"Brida, go after that man. I want to question him."

Without a word his sister bolted for out and sped down the sidewalk, a grin of anticipation on her face. She loved nothing better than running down an absconding fellow. With that bit of business concluded, Eidan turned his full attention to his woman. She'd raised her arm in an effort to dislodge his grip, and he narrowed his eyes.

"Why are you trying to leave?"

"Am I under arrest?"

"Of course not." Perhaps she should be, at least then he'd know where she was. Once they reached a new accord between them and he'd had several days of intimate contact with her, he had faith she'd be more docile and he could leave her unattended without worry of abduction or harassment. Especially since he now had most of the settlement's organized crime structure behind mag bars with no bail or hearing on the horizon. Plus his incapacitating malaise had disappeared completely. He felt like a new man.

"Let me go." She jerked forcibly, and he automatically tightened his grip. Her eyes widened, and she let out a gasp. He released her immediately, concerned he'd inadvertently injured her in his overwhelming drive to keep her close so he could explain away his atrocious behavior. She had to forgive him.

"How dare you touch me?" Teah jutted out her chin and glared at him, outraged and closed-off to him in a way he'd never seen before. His belly went cold. This reconciliation might not proceed so easily after all. "After all I've been through, you think you can maul me."

What had she been through? He'd been so shocked to see her suddenly there, apparently unharmed and filled with the defiance he'd come to expect, he hadn't stopped to think about what circumstances she might have suffered in the past twenty or so hours. He tried to soften his voice. "What happened to you, my sweet?"

"I'm not your sweet. I'm not your anything." With that she spun on her heel and fled the station, the ill-fitting door closing slowly behind her retreating figure.

His sinking belly went cold with dread, and once again his head ached in time with the rapid beats of his heart. He'd handled all of this so badly, he was beginning to doubt he'd be able to make things right. Without Teah, what was he left with?

****

At least Broose had missed her. Teah shook out her mussed hair and let the aircuttle gather up the strands as he hovered close to her head, his little exhalations of contentment nearly continuous. She urged herself to calm, her slight ordeal was over, finally safe at home with the door locked behind her. She'd checked on the animal and then the postal office as soon as she'd left the security station, and the incredibly irritating sheriff. She'd even managed to open the service counter for the remainder of the day. No one had come by to pick up or drop off, so it seemed a wasted effort, but still, she regained a certain calm in doing her duty again.

Throughout the shift she'd expected Eidan to come crashing through the door, grabbing and demanding, but he'd never appeared. Perhaps he was finally accepting she wasn't going to be a plaything to be discarded and then picked up whenever it amused him.

As soon as she could bring herself to close up shop, she did, the poor night's sleep and stress she'd suffered over the past day finally catching up to her and making her shake with exhaustion and anxiety. She carefully made her way up to her apartment and was greeted by an excited Broose, who acted as if he'd forgotten she'd just seen him two hours before.

"Do you want to go out? I'm sorry I was gone and you were locked up last night."

The aircuttle floated closer and stroked her ear with the edge of one of his tentacles. His big black eye stayed locked on hers as he shaded his skin from violet to pale blue then back again. She went to the door and forced herself to open it, suddenly fearful that one of Bokum's goons had avoided capture and was now waiting outside her door, anxious for revenge against the woman who'd been the trigger for his boss's downfall. No one was near her building that she could see in the evening shadows. Broose fluttered past her and hovered over the landing as he spun and surveyed the night.

"Go on, have fun. Come back in the morning!" The aircuttle seemed to agree as he twined his tentacles on the railing then stretched them out as he rose. With a scraping sound he let go and shot up into the sky, soon invisible to her gaze. Alone again. She supposed she could track down Dorian for company, but then she'd have to explain where she'd been, and likely endure more of his warnings. Not worth it.

Shivering with the recurrence of fear that something malignant out in the gathering dark was coming for her, she quickly retreated to her apartment and locked the door. A shower might calm her, and she certainly would feel better after cleaning off the distress of the past day.

She dropped her soiled clothes in the hamper and retreated to her bathroom, running hot water and letting steam fill the air. As soon as she stepped inside the shower stall and the warm water pummeled her skin, she let out a deep sigh and rotated slowly, allowing the spray to work against her tense shoulders, aching back, and sore thighs. She rubbed soap into her hair, the skin of her arms, then lathered her chest and breasts, all the while demanding her tired mind not to dredge up any memory of how Eidan's hands had felt on her, how her body leaped to arousal and readiness with his every caress and rumbled demand. He'd somehow managed to reach a part of herself she'd never know she possessed, the part that wanted to be cared for, directed by someone she knew was acting in her best interest. In the end, he'd discarded her and she doubted she'd ever be able to surrender to another man the way she had with Eidan. Probably for the best, since no man could match him.

Sniffing back a sigh of sadness, she turned off the refreshing water and stepped from the shower, wrapping a thick towel around her body and another around her freshly washed hair. A dull thumping noise caught her attention as she wrapped the towel more tightly around her head. Was someone trying to break in?

Fighting her first instinct to call Eidan for help, she instead exited the bathroom and rushed to her wall monitor, her wet feet slipping slightly on the smooth floor. She reminded herself to order a rug or two at the first opportunity, but such mundane thoughts were driven from her mind when she saw Eidan Cozad at her door, his fist raised to administer another resounding blow.

Her skin went cold, then bloomed hot. Anger boiled up, and she jabbed her finger at the voice link so hard she bent the digit back to a painful angle. "What are you doing out there?"

"Let me in, Teah. Right now."

She shook her head, then realized he couldn't see her denial. "Absolutely not."

"I know your security code."

Her throat tightened as she took this in, but quickly decided bravado was necessary. "I changed my numbers."

"You didn't." He sounded so arrogant, so sure of himself and her that she wanted to throw something at him. But she'd have to open to door to gain a target.

"You wouldn't dare. That would be illegal entry, forced invasion, intimidation of a Collective representative..." She trailed off, unable to come up with more preemptive allegations to hurl at him.

He growled, literally growled like he had earlier at the security station when he'd run off Venture. As it had before, her pussy swelled and dampened at the sound. No, she wasn't going to be aroused by him and his masculine posturing.

Just as she took in a deep and, she hoped, calming breath, her door flew open and he stepped inside, all two meters of muscular and determined Eleoni male. His narrowed eyes took in her nearly bare body, and he tightened his jaw as he kicked the door shut behind him. She clutched her towel close and stumbled back a step. The thick pile of the fabric pulled against her tight nipples.

"Leave. You aren't welcome here."

"I don't need you to welcome me. I need you to listen to me."

Teah fought the childish urge to clap her hands over her ears. If she did, her towel would likely fall off. Not that seeing her bare body would be a novel experience for him, he'd already mapped every centimeter of it.

"I need to know you're unharmed. All I can think about is what might have happened to you." Eidan's voice deepened, and he took a step her way, his gaze taking in her bare, unblemished limbs and she wished the towel would suddenly stretch to conceal her entirely.

"There's no need for your concern. I'm perfectly fine. It turns out kidnapping is not as terrible as you might imagine." She forced as much confidence and surety into her voice as she could muster. He shook his head once and moved closer.

"You didn't go to medical for a checkup as you should have."

"I wasn't injured. Why would I take up their time? Why did they tell you I hadn't been there? It's none of your business."

"I've told you before, the safety and security of everyone in this settlement is most definitely my business." Now he was close enough to touch and her pussy was wet well beyond the dampness left behind by the shower. He reached for the edge of the towel, and she flinched back.

"What do you think you're doing?"

"A more thorough visual inspection."

"I'm not your property. I'm not yours to assess." Her tough words ended in a squeal of surprise as he took hold of her covering and tugged gently. Her body flared with heat at the nearness of his hands, and she blinked back sudden tears of hurt and longing. It wasn't fair he was here, pressing her, when she'd been abducted and had to hold her own against a wily criminal, all after Eidan had rejected *her*. It was too much.

His hand came to rest on her side, his thumb under the flap of towel. He was warm and strong, and she wanted nothing more than to lean into him and tell him all about her time with Venture. "Why are you here? You don't want me any longer. You made that perfectly clear—"

"Shut up."

Her mouth clamped shut with shock, and she stared up at him, unable to believe he'd said something so rude in such a quiet tone. His violet eyes held hers as his mouth tightened briefly. "I need you to listen to me, please listen, and don't argue right away. *Please*."

The quiet entreaty in his voice brought her near automatic deflection to a quick halt. At her silence, he closed his eyes briefly and sighed, then met her gaze again, his jaw clenched.

"I was wrong to push you away. I was … afraid of what was happening and thought if we were apart, it would stop. But it didn't. It got worse, and when I realized you were gone … taken…" He sighed again, shuffled closer, his hand rubbing along the towel absently. "Tell me you're all right."

Teah swallowed hard. She wasn't all right. She was completely confused. "You aren't afraid of anything."

"I'm afraid of how I feel."

His answer was so quiet she could barely hear it. Just as she prepared to ask how he felt, he swayed and sank to his knees in front of her. Before she could react, his arms circled her hips and he pressed his face to her belly. Taken by surprise, it was all she could do to thread her fingers through his warm hair and listen to him.

"I'm so sorry I treated you so callously. You were wonderful to me as I recovered, and I owe you everything. Forgive me."

Her heart ached for him and her own fresh grief. She buried her fingers deeper in his hair, the silky strands tickling her palms. He tightened his grip and shifted against her, his nose pressing directly into her belly button. She understood fear, understood how confusing and overwhelming it had been between their rushed relationship and his terrible injury.

"I forgive you." It was easy to say, easy to mean, and as soon as she uttered it, a dark part of her heart lightened. Even if nothing else came to pass between them, at least they'd made amends.

"I'm sorry you were taken. You had to be so frightened. I need you to know I did everything I could to find you." At this he looked up at her, his eyes filled with remorse and she stroked her fingertips along his beard, curving them around his chin.

"I know you did. I was all right, truly. He treated me very politely—"

He sucked in a breath and narrowed his eyes. "It *was* that man at the station. I knew he was the one—"

"Hired to do a job and he was completely professional. He never hurt me or said a harsh word. I even taught him to knit a bit." She wanted to forestall any vendetta against Venture. She hoped the charmer was long gone and she and Eidan could forget about the incident. He scowled and released his grip on her waist to run his fingers down her arms as if looking for any minor contusion that would prompt a trans-galactic pursuit. "I want you to let him go."

"He's gone. Brida's quite put out she let him escape the planet." Eidan rubbed at her wrists like he thought she'd been bound. "Why did you want him to get the reward?"

"I was angry with you and it seemed like a good way to hurt you."

Eidan's expression lightened slightly, and he curved his hands around her hips. The towel slipped, and she didn't mind. "Petty. I wouldn't have thought that of you."

"I'm not so nice. I've told you that before."

"You're nice enough for me." His words lingered, and she wasn't sure what he meant.

She was still reeling but had a feeling the answer to one question would steady them both.

"What do you want from me, Eidan?"

He shuddered out a huge breath and rubbed his face along the towel now slipping dangerously down her chest. She stopped it before her breasts were exposed and straightened her back. If he just wanted a body to have sex with, she needed to know. Her feelings for him were too deep and strong to withstand being a mere bedmate. It would destroy her to mean so little to him.

"Do you still love me or did I kill that by being a fool?"

He remembered her blurted endearment. She bit her lip, not quite sure what to say. The truth, it always had to be the truth with Eidan. He was too astute for her to deceive. "I do."

He looked up, and she slid her hands along his shoulders as he spread his fingers over the thick fabric covering her buttocks. Something burned in his gaze and she struggled to breathe. "It's more to me."

More than love? What did that even mean? Before she could ask for clarification, he continued.

"I'm sick with it, Teah. My body is changing for yours. I can't sleep, I can't eat, I can't think." He punctuated his tortured litany by grabbing at her hand and pressing hard kisses to the skin of her wrists and up to her elbows, his beard tickling her skin even though she knew to expect the prickles.

"Please be with me." There was an ache in his voice that made her heart contract.

"Tonight?"

"Whatever you can give me."

****

He wanted to beg for forever, but he'd barely been able to ask for a few hours. He stared up at her, completely in thrall to Teah, and some newly minted part of his soul reveled in the vulnerability. Always before he'd kept up his guard, had never considered being at someone else's mercy, whether with his body or heart, yet here he knelt, surrendering all of himself to a human woman he'd just met. He had no choice, his very cells revolting against him when he left her.

Her expression was as soft as when she soothed her orphaned pet, and his body lit with the fire of hope. The brief taste of her skin lingered on his tongue and he wanted to rip the heavy towel from her body and suck on her fingertips, nipples, and clit, every sensitive little part of her that might make her shudder and sigh.

She ran her thumb across his cheek, and he shivered at the tenderness of the gesture. But she still hadn't invited him to stay, let alone indicated she felt at all inclined to allow him any intimacies. A fresh wave of relief that she was safe, that he knew where she was once again filled him in a cool wave of pleasure. Even if she asked him to leave, if he never touched her again, he'd know she was alive and experiencing a life with joys and challenges as she deserved.

"Will you?"

"Will I what?"

"Allow me to stay?"

A tiny smile flirted around her lips. "I'm used to you issuing orders, not asking permission."

"It feels more like I'm begging." He couldn't resist that little bit of humor, taking the chance it would not go amiss. In all truth, he was pleading with her for the future he wanted.

The smile faded, and she blinked her eyes a few times. "You can stay."

A tremendous wave of happiness bubbled up inside, tempered by a rush of sexual anticipation. Yes, he wanted to hold her tight and protect her from the galaxy, and he wanted to bury himself deep inside her warmth where he could lose all concerns by pleasing her.

"Stand up," she urged him with little tugs on his arms, but he resisted, liking looking up at her and seeing the flush of excitement color her cheeks.

"Come down."

With a sigh she acquiesced, sinking to her knees in front of them as her coverings came askew. He resolutely kept his eyes locked on her face. This wasn't the time to leer. He cupped one hand around her cheek, and she pressed against his palm. "I'm glad you're here."

Taking that as the best sort of invitation, he leaned toward her and met her for a sweet kiss, more chaste than any he'd experienced since his very first many years ago. Teah didn't part her lips or use her tongue, but instead met his soft caresses with her own. She moved against him and somehow was straddling his lap, the towel covering her body falling to the floor. His palms found the warm silkiness of her skin, skimming down the slender line of her back, coming to rest on the full globes of her ass. She curved to him, her mouth still sweetly closed against his.

Forgoing the haven of her kiss, he drew back and gave her a look. A much warmer welcome than he'd hoped for. His whole body seemed warmer, more energized like he'd taken a swift jolt of some amphetamine. She licked her lips and tilted her hips his way.

"What were you planning on doing this evening?"

Another little smile flashed and she tilted her head to one side. The towel wrapped around her temples slipped, and he pulled it free, tossing it aside before gathering up a hank of her damp hair in his fingers. He drew it to his nose and sniffed in the light floral fragrance he remembered.

"I've already washed my hair, which was my major goal." She stroked along his shoulders and let her hands come to rest alongside his neck.

"I would have enjoyed performing that task for you."

"Really? My arms get so tired when I do it." She leaned back slightly, as if to show how exhausted she was, and he allowed himself to look over her luscious body. No bruises or contusions, so he allowed the idea of hunting Venture down and breaking a few of his bones to fade. Teah wanted the miscreant to scuttle away unharmed, so he'd allow it this time. It she was ever in danger again, nothing would stay him from exacting whatever revenge he decided to seek.

"Shall I take on the task tomorrow morning?" It was a bold assertion, and one Teah might take offense to, considering their tentative rapprochement.

She laughed then, one of those familiar laughs he'd missed more than he wanted to admit. "It would be too soon, I'm afraid it wouldn't take kindly to it. Frizzy and unsightly."

He'd love it however it looked.

"Why are we talking about hair?"

"What else would you care to talk about?"

"I'd like to discover other ways I might be of service to you tonight, since it seems your personal grooming needs have been satisfied." This gentle teasing between them pleased him in a way he'd never experienced. He trusted her to understand his intentions, to relax into the ebb and flow of their shared conversation, not having to hold back or calculate the impact of his words. It was odd to think he would find that with a woman of another race, but find it, he had.

Teah furrowed her brow as if in deep thought. "I'm rather self-sufficient, as a rule."

"In all things?" He wanted her to need him, wanted her to be as desperate to be with him as he was for her. She wasn't melded to him, and knowing she lacked this molecular bind left him a bit insecure. More than a bit, he was as terrified about it as he would be in a failing ship spiraling out of orbit toward a sun.

She gave an impatient shake of her head, a damp tendril of hair sliding along her neck, and tightened her grip on his arms. "Stars, Eidan Cozad, I'm completely naked and sitting in your lap. If you can't think of what I'd like to do with you this evening—"

He cut off her declaration with a kiss, but one that was deep and searching, one she returned with equal fervor. Her scent filled his nose as her tongue slid along his. She whispered his name against his cheek and nuzzled into his beard like she couldn't get close enough to him.

"I didn't want to presume."

"I want you to presume all over me." Her voice was rough as she gave him permission.

Again he grasped her full hips and she scooted even closer, the cleft of her pussy hot and soft against his thickening cock. She rocked, and he could feel the hard nubs of her engorged nipples through the material of his shirt. Wriggling in his arms, she eased a hand between their bodies and stroked him through his trousers. His response was shocking and immediate. Every glauca on his body pebbled and sent tiny pulses of electricity through his nerve endings, all the tiny stimulations combining in a wave of sensation that almost overcame him. He hadn't really needed further proof of his meld, but this coordinated pleasure was something he'd never experienced before.

He drew back from her, a little dizzy with the new experience.

"What?" Teah whispered in his ear. "Am I too heavy?"

He tightened his grip on her, unwilling for her to move even a millimeter away. "No. It's just that my glauca are reacting in a way…"

"Painful? Should I stop?" She slid her hand to his lower abdomen and studied him with darkened eyes.

"No, keep touching me, please."

Rhythmic strokes began again, her palm sliding luxuriously up and down the underside of his cockhead. She told him to take off his clothes and he did, his hands clumsy as he struggled with his shirt. As soon as he'd pulled it clear, Teah lowered her mouth to the line of spots that curved across his chest and gave them a long, steady lick. The jolt of pleasure that shot through him nearly levitated his body from the floor. He'd had no idea the power a meld could have over his body. "I'm sorry!"

She took her mouth from his nipple where she'd been vigorously sucking. "Why are you sorry?"

"You don't have these marks. You can't feel what I'm feeling," he gasped out, dizzy with arousal and joy. It wasn't fair for her to be denied this amplified sense of completion and satisfaction. Should he explain what had happened? Later, when he was more rational. Now was the time for passion.

"It's better than before?" She stopped stroking his cock and instead went to work on the fastener to his trousers, her bare body curled against his in beautiful lines of thigh, hip, belly, and breast.

"It does, it's more intense than … oh." Eidan couldn't stop the sigh that left him when she freed his cock from the confining garments, or the moan he couldn't help but give when she reclined against his thighs and took him in her hot mouth. He leaned back on his hands and watched as she slowly licked at his tip, her gaze flickering up to his, then lowering as she reached to tug his pants off his hips. Before he realized her intentions, she stroked her thumbs along the glauca that circled the tops of his thighs and simultaneously sucked half his length into her mouth. His hips jerked up, and he shouted out. His climax roiled in close like a storm about to hit and he ordered her to stop her activities.

She released his cock after running her tongue along the slit at the tip and he thought he might spill all over her face, but he restrained himself. She was panting, and he fancied he could see moisture gleaming in the curls between her legs. "What do you want?"

"My mouth on you. Now." He ground it out, holding on to control with all his might.

"Lie down. I'm not stopping." Her voice hitched as she levered herself up on her hands and knees and crawled over his body, her mouth caressing his cock in fits and starts until she'd straddled him, her knees on either side of his head. He leaned up and tongued her damp pussy, searching for her clit amid the slick folds, hoping he could bring her to orgasm before he did. Her delicious scent overwhelmed him. As if she understood his needs, Teah slowed her kisses, merely resting her lips against his cockhead until he found her full nub. Her body jerked and he ran the flat of his tongue along it, taking in her tangy moisture as she suckled steadily at his cock.

He grasped at her ass cheek to hold her still and allowed his thumb to press against her rear hole. She stopped her caress and spoke.

"Yes, just a little."

Happy to abide by her request, he rubbed against the ring of muscle and she rocked her hips in time as she returned her attention to his cock. Their steady movements against each other soon synchronized, and he listened to the happy little squeaks she made, the sounds vibrating along his shaft. His balls contracted and he panted against her wet pussy as his skin shivered with heat. She knew he was coming and pulled him deeper in her mouth, sucking steadily. He tried to find her clit again, but the rapid tremors of his muscles as his climax rocked through him made him fall away from her and he groaned loudly. Heat coursed out of his balls and jetted into her mouth as he released, his whole body straining with the effort.

Wave after wave of tingling pleasure rippled over him, and he fell back with a sigh, too replete to move even though he knew she was tense with unfulfilled need.

"Teah, I'm sorry—"

"You keep apologizing for nothing. You think I don't feel wonderful when you touch me? You think I'm not going to come as hard and fast as you just did?" She was almost breathless as she rolled away from him and then arranged one of her thighs across his heaving chest as she faced him. She scooted forward and spread her legs wider so he could turn his head and see all of her slippery pink sex. She worked two fingers against herself and her head lolled back as her legs quivered.

He remained a fascinated bystander for a few seconds, then sat up, holding her legs as he encouraged her to lie back and relax. She collapsed into a beautiful heap, and he watched her fingertips swirl among her folds. Her little pants evolved into gasps of his name. His cock wasn't up to the challenge at the moment so his fingers would have to do. He slid one inside her tight opening, and she wailed and twitched, begging for more. He withdrew the first finger, then pressed two digits against the dent of her opening. Her eyes flew open, and she nodded rapidly even as she stroked her clit with rapid little circles. She took him in, took him as willingly as she did everything else for him. He crooked his fingers inside her warmth, and she bucked against the floor, her low cry of building pleasure suddenly erupting into a sob as she shuddered violently.

He pulled her across his chest and listened to her racing breaths. She draped one limp arm across his shoulder and sighed deeply. He relaxed in the euphoric sensations for a moment, but the hard floor under his body began to intrude on his thoughts.

"Should we go to your bed?"

She rose up on one elbow and gave him a sharp look. "If we go into the bedroom you're going to want to get that gorgeous cock of yours inside me."

"My recovery time, while more rapid than for any other male, is not quite up to that task yet." She smirked at his poor pun and settled back against his body. "Still, I want to ask you a few things without being distracted by the possibility."

"Ask away, all my defenses are down."

He threaded his fingers in her hair and considered her defenses. Teah was smart, a hard worker, and tough enough to manage living in this nearly lawless place, but she also showed him humor and compassion in addition to an apparent appreciation of his sexual practices. He needed to know her intentions, since his were now embedded in his genetic code. He would only be able to shed his meld with her with a long, grieving withdrawal, or a powerful chemical concoction administered over several weeks.

"I want to chip you." *Need to chip you.*

She craned her neck around and stared up at him with a puzzled frown. "What are you talking about?"

He could lie and say he was pondering mortality due to his recent close call and her just resolved peril, but that would be cowardly. He needed to explain what was happening, that since she lacked Eleoni DNA, she wasn't able to bind as completely to him as he was to her, and therefore he needed a way to find her at any time, just to reassure himself of her location and safety. All Eleoni wore chips. Mothers synchronized theirs to their children's, and doing so was the first formal step in confirming a meld between lovers.

"A small transponder system, self-perpetuating in your cells. So I can find you."

She rose from his body, her breasts bouncing slightly as she sat up and stared down at him, her features drawn in serious lines. "You're joking. You want to add some tracking device to my *body*?"

He wasn't sure where her outrage was originating. It was a gesture of love and trust, the most meaningful component to serious courtship he could attempt. "Of course I do. What kind of a man do you take me for?"

She lurched to her feet and jammed her slim hands on her hips. He looked up at her from the floor, one side of his brain very appreciative of the unique view of her pubis, belly, and breasts, the other desperately trying to regroup and gain control of the conversation. It was difficult to reconcile the two sides.

"A man who wants to track my every move, apparently."

"I want to keep you safe." It was difficult to converse from his prone position so he rose and faced her. "If you'd been mine from the first, I would have taken you from that scoundrel before he could have said three words."

He was able to admit Teah's apparent regard for the kidnapper still rankled, if only to himself.

"Yours from the first?" She cocked her head back as if he'd said something insane, and with cool shock, realization dawned. Humans didn't meld, humans didn't chip, humans didn't follow any of the civilized rituals of love his people did. She was taken aback. "You don't own me, Eidan Cozad."

But you own me, he wanted to reply, again experiencing that low-level panic that his enamored state was in no way reflected in her feelings for him. In an effort to collect his thoughts, he took a breath and frowned, which was apparently the wrong approach to take.

"Are you going to argue with me about this? I'm not having you put additives inside my body. No discussion." At this she gathered up her towels and wrapped them around her body. "Do you have them—no, forget that, I don't want to know."

"Every Eleoni has them. They are administered to babies along with immunizations."

"Babies? You put trackers in *babies*?" Her voice rose in a disbelieving wail, and her mouth fell open. "Doesn't that hurt? Why would a mother allow it?"

Eidan willed away his urge to defend his culture to a human, whose collective impulses seemed to center on self-centeredness and grubbing for profit. He took a step towards Teah, desperate for her to not move away. She stayed put, her eyes blazing up at him in outrage. He cautiously extended a hand her way, and she let him rest it on her shoulder. She was trembling.

"It's a loving act. It facilitates an even stronger bond and provides an additional layer of security as the child grows."

She made a slightly mollified huffing sound. "But why would you do that to me? I'm not a child, and I don't think I'll be kidnapped again. Not since you've made your case against Bokum and incarcerated the lot of them."

He ventured an arm around her waist, and she took a hesitating step his way, still staring at him and waiting for an answer. How was he going to explain something everyone like him already knew as a fact as immutable as gravity?

"I need you to be linked to me in some way, even if all I can manage is an artificial bond." There, he'd said it and now could only wait for her response. He'd always be hers.

"But I am linked to you. I love you." Teah pressed her lips together and studied him intently. "I know you don't love me, but—"

"What are you talking about?" Confusion sent his mind into a static-filled state.

"I know Eleoni have this meld thing that binds a couple together. We don't have it, and it would be impossible to achieve. I'm not Eleoni. End of story. I suppose that chip is your way of trying to make it up to me. I appreciate it, but you don't have to. I love you, and I'll be true to you no matter what."

She drew in a shuddering breath and squared her shoulders. Ready for whatever came her way.

"I didn't know you were aware of the phenomenon."

"Someone recently brought it to my attention."

Not Brida, she would have said something to him if she had. No matter, he could repair whatever feeling of inadequacy Teah had entertained since learning of it. "So you know an Eleoni's cells change, when he falls in love. It's an unstoppable force which creates many layers of interdependence that grow over time. Initially there are physical indicators, like overwhelming well-being when in each other's presence and symptoms of illness when parted. Lovers also synch their chips, the tighter to bind themselves to each other. Over the years, the meld produces a low-level telepathy and promotes longevity."

Teah frowned and shook her head. "So if you're with me, you won't live as long?"

Why couldn't he communicate this miracle to her? "I'll live a long life and so will you."

"If being with me cuts you off from your natural potential, I'll go so you can find an Eleoni woman who's right for you. I can't have you sacrifice it for—"

He cut her off with a kiss, cupping his hand around the back of her head to keep her in place. Teah softened and drew close as she always did and he nearly sank back into foreplay, but instead gave himself a tremendous mental shake.

"*Alati*, listen. I've melded with you. You are the person I'm meant to be with. I have terrible headaches when we are separated, my glauca have already attuned to your touch, the process is underway in my very cells to bind me to you. It's beyond love, what I feel for you."

She blinked, and her mouth fell open. One small step his way and she was fully in his embrace. "How is that possible?"

Delight that she seemed to be accepting the situation filled him with warmth and hope. "I don't know. I've never heard of it happening between our races, but I haven't made a study of it either."

"But I would be like a communicator with no receiver. You are going through all these changes while I stay the same. There would be none of this telepathy, or…"

Tiny frown lines appeared on her forehead as she trailed off. Eidan's body, already attuned to her presence, had warmed and tensed as soon as they'd begun touching. He wanted her again, even if his body wasn't ready.

"Wait. What did you say about headaches and feeling ill?"

He kissed her cheek and nosed into her damp hair, scented like her very essence. Her breasts rubbed against his chest, and he reveled in how utterly perfect it was to be with her. "Those are the usual symptoms of a new meld, when parties are separated. Right now I feel in the peak of health."

His cock thrummed a reminder it would like to be attended to in the near future.

Teah put a hand to her head. "Nausea, too?"

Eidan nodded, contentment filling him as he accepted the idea he might have a future with her. She loved him and wanted to be with him. He didn't need more than that. They'd manage without a full meld. After all, every other sentient species accomplished it.

Teah sagged in his arms with a moan. Alarmed, he carefully sat her on the edge of her bed and gathered a blanket around her. "Do you need something? Some water?"

The flush he'd given her had drained from her face. "I need to see a doctor."

Fear blasted through all the hard-won happiness, and Eidan knelt in front of her to gather up her cool hands. He'd get them dressed, but first wanted to assess her condition. "What's wrong?"

"You did it to me. You're so damned domineering you made me change!" Teah's voice rose up in a wail, and Eidan sat back on his heels, shocked at her display of unhappiness.

"I don't understand. But I'll get you to the clinic." Gathering himself, he kissed her palms, then rose to collect his clothes. Teah hadn't been wearing anything other than a towel, so he'd have to invade her closet.

With a harsh cry, she fell back against the bed, and he rushed to her side. She'd flung one arm over her eyes and her shoulders shook with sobs. Desperate to comfort her, he stroked her hair and whispered her name. Perhaps he should call for a pick-up. Teah abruptly flung her arm away and glared at him, her cheeks bright pink again. What was happening to her?

"You're a real pain, do you know that?"

Speechless at her anger, all Eidan could do was nod. He had behaved shabbily in the past.

"Here I've been thinking I might have a brain tumor or some weird virus and it was you all along." Teah punctuated this tirade with a finger poked directly in the center of his chest, narrowly missing one of his still-tender scars.

"What did I do?"

With a huff Teah sat up and pushed at him, but he refused to be budged. She had a lot of strength for one suddenly taken ill. "Melding! You got me. I'm all messed up, apparently forever. More like being kidnapped without knowing it."

The pieces clicked into place, and Eidan couldn't resist the smile that emerged. She was his, in the same manner he was hers. A miracle.

"Don't look so smug! Think you're so smart. Big, bossy man."

Her outrage barely concealed the happy light in her eyes, and she couldn't maintain her frown against the grin playing across her lips. His joy expanded and he wanted to laugh, to shout at the moon at the future they shared, but instead pulled her into his arms and bent over her.

"I know I'm smart, and strong. Filled with such male prowess I melded with an unwitting human. Made her mine."

Teah sputtered a wordless protest. . His blood rushed at the feel of her arms and legs brushing up against him. "You did. Proud of yourself?"

"Yes. Do you still want to see the doctor?"

She shook her head, her lovely hair fanning out over the sheets. He had to remember to brush it for her later. After he'd paid proper respects to her sex. "Rusk's doctor is human. What would he know about it?"

"It's really very simple. Stay close to me and we'll both feel fine."

Teah calmed, all her fuss and upset disappearing as she relaxed against him. "What about that chip thing?"

"I'd rest easier if you had one."

She drew one of his hands to her lips and kissed his knuckles. "Then I'll do it. Where will you put it?"

Relief washed over him. "I'll choose an especially tender spot." Teah had captured him, but he still needed to assert his will now and then.

"Only if you kiss it better." Teah laughed. "That's it then? We're together?"

Something in his chest loosened, and to his shock, Eidan felt tears prickle under his lids. Clearing his throat past the lump with had just emerged, he nodded. "We are."

Teah sighed as her expression softened. "More than love?"

"Beyond love, *alati*."

****

Teah sensed Eidan's contentment like a calming touch against her skin. She tried to focus on her driving, on the rare balmy conditions they were enjoying on this journey deep into the grasswoods, but what loomed ahead intruded in her mind. The columned trees swayed overhead, allowing bright beams of light to shine down on the narrow, muddy path she'd chosen.

"You're doing the right thing," Eidan rumbled as he reached out a hand to rest against her thigh. "He's ready to go."

Broose, two tentacles tightly wrapped around the shift lever to stay upright in the cart, blatted out a loud, excited breath. He had filled out in the past few weeks, and his color changes were more strident. Growing up. Time to rejoin his flock, or what was left of it.

"I know. It's just…"

"Painful. You'll miss him and worry about him," Eidan finished. Instead of being irritated when he completed her sentences, Teah was pleased. It was likely a feature of the meld and their growing interdependence, or perhaps it was simply a side product of being in love. It still sometimes took her by surprise, both the depth of her feelings, and Eidan's numerous expressions of devotion. She'd gone so long making her way on her own, it sometimes brought her up short how much she now counted on Eidan. Like this trip. She didn't know how she would have done it without him by her side.

Putting aside such thoughts, which would lead to her wanting to bed Eidan rather than applying herself to the task at hand, she slowed the cart and began to cast about for a familiar clearing. A few meters ahead, she recognized a distinctive fallen tree and stopped the vehicle. Broose immediately flew out the open window, and Teah's heart contracted with fear. Was he leaving already?

She struggled with the door latch and finally wrenched it open, stumbling out and peering overhead for any sign of the creature.

"He's over here," Eidan called out. Teah trotted to his side, sliding in the mud until he wrapped his arms around her. A pleasant wave of reassurance swept over her, and she leaned back into his chest. Broose hovered over a scrubby stand of nettlebush, his colors cycling scarlet and lime green in a wild display.

"He looks upset." Teah planted a foot in the mud and prepared to go to the aircuttle and offer him some reassurance. He was probably frightened of the strange environment. After all, he hadn't been back to this clearing since she'd rescued him after the massacre of his family. Maybe he was having flashbacks.

"Wait. I think I know what he's spotted," Eidan pulled her back and nosed in her hair.

Teah tried to relax her tense muscles as she peered at the rustling spines of the plant. A breeze sang in the top reaches of the surrounding grasswood, making the stalks rattle like the galaxy's largest windchimes. A bright purple flash captured her attention, and she stared, determined to make out whatever it was. A long tendril slowly rose out of the leaves, and Broose zipped over to it. He extended one of his tentacles and very gently tapped the waving appendage.

"I think it's another like him," Eidan whispered in her ear.

"Let's hope they don't fight."

A bulbous shape emerged from the spikes, morphing lavender and reshaping into a petite aircuttle with large, dark eyes riveted to Broose. Teah drew in a breath as the animals hovered together, slowly exchanging touches along their respective tentacles.

"Do you think that's a girl?" Humor lightened Eidan's tone and lifted her mood.

"I don't know. Broose might like boys, or aircuttles might be hermaphrodites for all I know."

Eidan chuckled, and the new aircuttle fluttered yellow for a second, but soon returned to inspecting Broose. "However they like to arrange their lives, it looks as if Broose has found a companion."

Both cuttles drifted up, appendages now intertwined. The breeze caught them and pushed the creatures out of sight into the waving canopy overhead. Pain twinged through Teah's heart, and she sighed. Broose was gone.

"I think he was grateful to you, Teah."

Turning in Eidan's arms, she ran her palms along his broad shoulders and rested her head on his chest. "I'm happy he thrived and could return to the wild, where he belonged."

Eidan slid his fingers down her back and cupped her buttocks in a knowing way. "I have to admit, it will be nice to visit you without him flapping in my face."

Teah laughed. "You were very patient with him."

"The reward of seeing you was well worth any obstacle I had to endure," Eidan replied. "It would have been difficult convincing you to move into my house with Broose objecting to having to share you with me every day."

Teah's heart, previously aching for her pet, underwent a tremendous wrench. "You want me to live with you?"

"I do. Unless you are worried about gossip." Despite Eidan's calm tone, she could sense his nervousness. Could he pick up on her surprise and happiness?

"I don't care what people think anymore." Teah tried to organize her thoughts. Waking up with him, sharing meals, planning a future together. What was there to object to? "What about Brida?"

Eidan smoothed some of her hair back. "She said to tell you she'd appreciate it if you'd hurry up so she can move out. Apparently, living with her brother has palled already."

Teah could well imagine Brida saying just that. "Well, if your sister needs my help, who am I to refuse?"

Suddenly she was swept up into the air and twirled around as Eidan hugged her tight. Laughing, she hung on until he'd calmed enough to put her down again. "I'll keep you from missing Broose, I promise."

"I'll hold you to that, Eidan Cozad." Teah met his delighted gaze, confident that this was just the beginning of the best part of her life.

The End

www.jjlore.com

Evernight Publishing

www.evernightpublishing.com